TRAPPED IN THE RUSSIAN ZONE

By Lorena Lefor Golke

Strategic Book Group

Strategic Book Group
P.O. Box 333
Durham, CT 06422
www.StrategicBookClub.com

ISBN: 978-1-60976-058-8

Book Design: Arlinda Van, Dedicated Business Solutions, Inc.

Acknowledgments

⁂

The author wishes to acknowledge **Ferdinand Golke and the Golke family** for this remarkable glimpse into the lives and trials of those who became displaced during the Second World War. Their story brings with it unparalleled insight into a significant period in history, at a time when eye witnesses to those events are passing from the scene.

The author also acknowledges the following individuals, whose vision, support, and technical insight contributed to the manuscript: Debra Gervais, Christopher Lefor, Terry Lefor, and Heather Beales.

Ferdinand Golke acknowledges:

My mother **Emma Breitkreutz Golke:** It was due to her high spirit and personal sacrifice that we made it to safety in the West together as a family. In spite of her personal affliction, she displayed remarkable resolve throughout our ten-year ordeal.

My sister **Herta (Golke) Holland** stood by me unconditionally as we were growing up, as well as during our trials when we were lost in a detainee camp. The steadfastness that Herta displayed was a source for which I drew strength and confidence. The fearlessness and determination Herta displayed in her youth, along with her committed support of our parents in their elder years, bears testimony to her remarkable strength of virtue and family dedication.

About the Author

Born in Canada during the depression the author Lorena Lefor was the eldest daughter in a family of eleven children. The family budget was limited and the chores unending, but Lorena managed to find time to write short stories about real people. She drew inspiration from her mother who believed that the real story is sometimes hidden in the shadows of time. Her mother's constructive influence went a long way in developing in Lorena a passion for real stories about real people.

Lorena married at a young age and in time gave birth to five children. Following the death of her husband in 1993, Lorena pursued her writing in earnest by attending the journalism program at Conestoga College in Kitchener, Ontario, a city that was once named Berlin. At this time Lorena uncovered her own German background and became interested in other unique experiences of immigrant families who had been displaced from Europe during the Second World War. Lorena's passion for the real story continues to inspire her writings. ... Contributed.

Foreword

Among the many experiences told by immigrant families from the 1940's, one of the most captivating accounts was that of the Golke family who found themselves in peril in Poland under the siege of WWII. Even though revisiting the pain of the past was difficult for them, my persistence and enthusiasm for the story eventually opened the way, resulting in many tales of greater significance than I had imagined. Each snippet of information they shared added to my determination to learn more about their experience and of the lives of those who had been uprooted by the boundaries of war.

"Trapped in the Russian Zone" chronicles the riveting true story of the Golke family through ten years of strife in their homeland and records their experience through the eyes of a child growing up in those troubled times. It gives a play by play account of their experience while living under occupation and their flight to safety that took them across the continent of Europe and through the Iron Curtain under unimaginable conditions and circumstances. The remarkable resourcefulness and determination of a young boy and his sister helped ensure the family's survival and adds a human touch to one of the most significant periods in history.

Table of Contents

Chapter One

Man from Volhynia

It was December 26, 1944, in the German-occupied Polish district of Warthegau in the small community of Shatenvaulde. On January 6, 1945, I was going to face trial by court-martial. I was only fifteen and had deserted the military during the peak of the war, and the Germans had zero tolerance for deserters. To be convicted of treason against Germany meant execution without mercy. I feared that I would not see my sixteenth birthday. We had come through a good deal to remain together, but now facing uncertainty I would soon leave my home and family and this time I would be going alone. My anxiety mounted with each passing day.

A harsh winter storm had set in. Four days had passed and Ferdinand remained housebound. Each day that passed meant one day closer to the inevitable fate that awaited him. The family had already sustained immeasurable losses. Emil Golke, Ferdinand's father and Emma's husband, had not returned home since his recruitment into the German army two years before, and the family knew nothing of his whereabouts. In the past Emma had been a pillar of strength, but today she spoke with deep concern.

"Your father may not return from the war," she said, "but losing you would be more than I could bear. You must leave soon, Ferdinand, before it is too late. The children and I will join you as soon as we are able."

After five days of confinement in the cabin, the storm finally broke. The wind had died down and the sun shone brightly in the sky. Ferdinand ventured out into the cold morning air. With only six days of freedom left before military guards would escort him to the guard post; he had no time to lose. There was one thing that Ferdinand must do. The thought of leaving his mother Emma and the children without wood for the fire in the depth of winter weighed heavily on his mind. He would sacrifice one more day to stack the wood by the cabin door. He knew that his father would expect him to.

Ferdinand could not bear the thought of disappointing his father even though his father might never return. As Ferdinand stacked the wood tightly against the wall of the cabin, the frost nipped his fingers through the frayed gloves that only partially covered his hands. An hour had passed and then two. His breath froze in the frosty air. He could endure the cold no longer. He stepped inside to warm himself by the large iron stove located in the middle of the room. Suddenly behind him the door of the cabin burst open and a man in uniform entered.

The man looked as though he had been engaged in battle. His appearance was frightful. The man's bearded face was covered with ice and snow, and the uniform he wore was tattered and torn. Fearing the man's intentions, Emma quietly waved Ferdinand from the room and sat the stranger by the fire. She offered him something to eat. He nodded his head but seemed unable to speak. He ravenously devoured what he had been given while the family waited in apprehension.

For some time the man remained silent as he sat. The heat from the iron stove melted the ice from the stranger's bearded face, and it was only then that Emma recognized him. He was Wolfgang Riece from Volhynia. Wolfgang, along with his wife Anna and their children, had lived in the same village with the Golkes back east. The Golkes had not seen the Riece family since 1939, the year that their village was evacuated.

The tale he told was frightening. "Emma," he said, "you are German and your lives are in danger. You must leave before it is too late. They are killing everyone in their tracks, and they will take no prisoners."

As a German soldier, Wolfgang had been engaged in combat with Russian troops just a few miles to the north until the situation became hopeless. The Golke family had no knowledge of the battle that had been waging for a number of days just a short distance from their door. Wolfgang fled west toward the German border but was unaware of his location when he arrived at the Golke's. His only thought was to make it beyond the border of Germany ahead of the Russians and to warn the villagers along the way. He begged for a change of clothes before departing. He deposited his tattered uniform in the fire, grabbed the loaf that Emma had wrapped for him and left the cabin.

Looking back over his shoulder, he repeated in a commanding voice, "Don't delay! Leave now!" he urged. "They will take no prisoners," he said as he disappeared in the same hurried manner in which he had come.

Ferdinand did not question the news. He knew being caught behind Russian lines would mean certain doom for all of them. Death by firing squad was no longer on the forefront of his mind. He thought of his mother who was defenseless against the fate that was now inevitable. He thought of his two younger sisters, Herta and Frieda, and his brother, Erich, who was not yet five. He knew in his heart that he would not abandon them. Safety now meant escaping into Germany over the Oder River. If they left now, in three days time they could reach the bridge over the Oder River ahead of the Russians.

As we prepared to leave I could not help thinking about how our lives had changed. It had been only five years since we had left Volhynia. I was just ten when we were loaded onto the boxcar in the cold of winter. Today it seemed so long ago. I had grown up, our family had changed, and my world had changed. Father had not returned from the war and if he were alive, there would be no hope of finding him. We would now be on the move again. Once again we would leave everything we owned except what we could carry and leave for the West.

Chapter Two

Displaced in the Land of Promise

Volhynia, Poland, was a vast territory to the southeast of Warsaw that stretched for hundreds of miles. The area had attracted German settlers from Prussia due to the fertile land and rich resources of timber to build homes. With the influx of Germans for hundreds of years the area was saturated by German influence. For two generations, the Golke family resided in Volhynia, Poland, in the village of Jachimufka. The new settlers from Prussia prospered, even though they remained displaced or without citizenship. From the time of Ferdinand Golke's birth in the spring of 1929, until he entered school for the first time in 1936, life in the village of Jachimufka was typical of village life in Poland. The people had larger families, celebrated family weddings and enjoyed holidays together. Every year in the fall everyone in the village celebrated the harvest.

The year 1929 was notably a challenging year on the world scene with the arrival of the Great Depression. It had been ten years since Poland had won political gains after the First World War; nevertheless there still remained an element of unrest among the people. In spite of the concerns of the times, the Golke family lived a simple life in the village. After leaving Prussia with very little money or possessions, the incoming German-speaking families appeared to thrive,

Volhynia
1795 ~ 1850
Golke family's sojurn from Prussia
(Center of German Culture)

even though the Great Depression had begun and the political scene was constantly changing.

While Ferdinand was growing up, his culture demanded
discipline. He had been taught that a boy had to work hard
and never cry. It simply wasn't masculine. Hard labor was
considered the only acceptable way to better oneself in life.
Anyone who would even suggest that there was an easier
way would be singled out as a lazy person. Convinced of that
philosophy, Ferdinand did his best to meet these expectations
and as the years passed, this discipline served him well.

1929–31 The Family Adds a New Member

The early years for Ferdinand were typical of most young
families in the village. The daily responsibilities of farm life
took his father from the house for most of his waking hours.

His mother Emma was by Ferdinand's side continuously. In 1931, at the age of two, the arrival of a younger sibling did not prove to be a pleasant experience for Ferdinand.

I was totally unprepared to share Mother's attention with anyone, never mind giving up my very own bed, since I was certain the new family member had arrived without an invitation. I made my disapproval known. In view of my persistent displeasure, I was confident that Mother would grow tired of her and give her back. To my distress, my protests fell on deaf ears.

Father made a new bed for me and placed it in the corner of the two room cabin. It was only then that I realized Mother was going to keep Herta after all. I felt wounded for a while, but before long I got used to the new bed, and I could hardly wait until Herta was old enough to play with me in the yard. In 1935, I was five years old and Herta was just over three and already she displayed spunk and a will of her own that rivaled mine. We played together for hours, and even though I had made many attempts I was never quite able to get the better of her. As the years went by, Herta and I became inseparable.

I enjoyed the continuous childhood bantering that was common between Herta and I, but Father had no patience for it. In one instance I had gotten a beating for tantalizing her. I was brokenhearted at the severity of my punishment. I decided to run away and hide in the field. I stayed there for a number of hours.

The day drifted into evening and young Ferdinand had not returned home. His father suggested that his mother go and find him and bring him home. Staying her ground on the matter, Emma insisted Emil should go, as he had inflicted the punishment.

Father was not what you would call a humble man, but in coming to bring me home I was convinced of his concern for me, even though he never uttered a word to mend my wounded heart. I was careful to avoid disappointing him again.

It was customary of the times to teach children responsibility at a young age. In the next few years Ferdinand began to prepare for his adult life, but he would have to learn many things before he would be allowed to go to school. Much would be expected of young Ferdinand. His sister Herta was too young to be given chores to do, but she was learning a great deal from being by her mother's side.

When I was not with Father, I helped Mother with the chores. My preference to help Mother taught me valuable skills that proved to be life-sustaining as future events unfolded. Discipline almost always came from Father and I can say that he took this job seriously. The relationship I had with Father for the most part was bittersweet.

Ferdinand was five years of age when he began to accompany his father on wood-cutting trips to the forest. In order to survive the harsh winters, he must learn how to fetch wood. By this time he had grown big enough to harness the horses. On one of the trips into the forest with his father, Ferdinand worked for several hours digging out tree stumps that they could salvage for winter wood. He paused for a short while with his father and sat beside him on a stump.

Ferdinand remarked, "Wouldn't it be wonderful Father if we could have this all of our life?" The remark made in innocence had caused his father to unexpectedly burst out in laughter. In misinterpreting his father's glee, Ferdinand hung his head in shame. He felt as though he had been rebuked. He would later learn that a time would come when even these simple things that he had spoken to his father about would be taken from them.

While we were still unaffected by the world scene, many things of significance to Poland were happening around us.

In the summer of 1932, Nazi candidates won 230 seats in the parliamentary election in Germany. Six months later the aging German president Paul von Hindenburg appointed Hitler as the new chancellor, ushering the Nazi Party into power and on February 28, 1933, the Nazi leader managed to manipulate von Hindenburg into declaring a state of emergency in Germany, suspending all guarantees of civil liberties.

Hitler approved of the strong-arm tactics of the newly appointed police chief of Munich, resulting in many being incarcerated to Dachau concentration camp. He continued to see the need for a network of concentration camps to be built. (The Master Plan by Heather Ann Pringle, Hyperion, New York)

In October 1939, the Polish province of Volhynia was annexed by Russia and has since disappeared from modern maps. Due to political adversity and changes in borders, Volhynia was gobbled up by Russia and is now part of the Ukraine.

1936–1939

In 1936 Ferdinand was seven years old and looking forward to attending school for the first time. Early in the spring of 1936, Emma contracted a painful and unsightly infection in her hands that prevented her from doing any of the household chores. Ferdinand became downhearted when he discovered that his mother's condition might prevent him from going to school. He had looked forward to going to school, but in those days the home life came first. Acquiring an education was not yet considered a priority. He had no way of knowing that difficult times were coming and much of what he was able to learn at home during this time would prepare him for the future when his life would depend on it. From this time on, Ferdinand's childhood came to an end.

Emil worked in the field from daylight until dark and was unable to assist in the household chores. This left Ferdinand to fulfill his mother's role. For a period of several months Ferdinand could not leave his mother's side. Under her critical eye, he stood on a stool to wash the dishes and the clothes. He learned to sew on buttons, peel potatoes, and start the cooking fires for the family meals. There was firewood to gather and the farm animals to be fed and watered. When he finished the inside chores he brought his father lunch in the field. He was severely chastised if anything went amiss. Ferdinand resented having to grow up so soon and missed being able to play with Herta in the childhood games they played.

The malady that had plagued the family had not deterred their attending services at the local church. This of course did not include children. It was customary to teach children godliness at home. In most cases Emil and Emma's absence from the home while attending church had no consequence, and they arrived home to find the household in order. There would only be one exception.

During our parents' absence, Herta and I decided to surprise them with a basket of cherries from the tree in the yard. I boosted Herta up the tree to pick the cherries that were not within reach. While climbing down from the tree, Herta broke her arm. She cried so hard that I was certain that she would die. I knew nothing of what to do but merely attempted to comfort her."

Even though we expected the arrival of our parents soon, I was faced with a dilemma for which I had not been prepared. I helped Herta into the cradle and rocked her to sleep. After our parents returned, I was sure that I would get a beating, but instead both Father and Mother focused their full attention on Herta.

Herta was taken to a doctor in the village but was turned away with the claim that it had begun to heal and nothing could be done. In order to correct the unsightly disfigurement, the arm would have to be rebroken. Emma did not give up however, for surely the crippling appearance of the arm would have lifelong consequences.

Emma sought out a woman in the village who was known for setting broken bones. She prepared Herta, carefully helping her into the wagon, and then she drove the team of horses into town. Even though Emma was desperate, she waited respectfully until after the church service to beg the woman for her help. Aghast at the appearance of the arm, the woman felt pity for this young girl. With no remedy for pain, the woman covered the arm in goose fat and began to massage it lightly for several minutes. With a sudden jerk, the arm was instantly reset and a splint was applied to keep the arm rigid. Herta's scream could be heard down the street. In time, Herta's arm healed and she no longer complained, which Ferdinand was extremely grateful for. Herta was rewarded with a new dress.

Chapter Three

Pandemonium Begins

(October 25, 1936. Mussolini and Hitler form the Rome-Berlin Axis. This constituted a political alliance between Germany and Italy.) In August 1939, Hitler from Germany and Stalin from Russia, signed a non-aggression pact which was intended for the purpose of carving up Poland between them. After Germany's advance, Russia annexed the eastern part of Poland, including Volhynia, and the "Exchange" began.

Ferdinand was seven years old in the fall of 1936, and with the family crisis under control, he attended school for the first time. The school system in Poland was authoritarian, with rules about behavior, punctuality, and adherence to a strictly controlled curriculum. The well-known expression "taught to the tune of the hickory stick" was applied without mercy. The teacher's authority went unchallenged. In spite of this, Ferdinand loved school and learned quickly. In his first years at school, Ferdinand learned to read and write in the Polish language.

I made many new friends at school, many of whom remained in my memory throughout my life. There were Gerhard and Frieda Radky, Helmet Schindler, Erna Dalke, and her younger brother Franc. My mother's youngest brother, Rudolf Breitkreutz, who was my uncle though he was only one year older than I was, also attended the small one room country school in Volhynia. There also was one special friend that I remembered the most; a girl named Erna Shmitkey. Her birthday was only a day before mine. I developed a special fondness for Erna, and even though she was a friend in my childhood, she captivated my thoughts continuously. Some of my fondest memories of my childhood included Erna when she would accompany her mother for visits to our home. I looked forward to their visits, when the three of us, Herta, Erna, and I were sent out to play, while the two mothers talked of matters too adult for our tender ears. The memory of my childhood friendship with Erna remained with me throughout my life.

The spring of 1937 came with the arrival of a new sibling. We named the baby Frieda, and for a short while the new baby took up all of our attention. With Herta as my constant companion, I no longer had a problem adjusting to a new addition to the family. I joined in with the others in assisting in her care. It was Herta who must now give up her bed. This she did without protest.

By the fall of 1937 rumors of war circulated throughout our rural village. As the political scene changed, so did Father's demeanor. The ever present fear of being drafted loomed over our household. As a German national, Father was expected to respond to the call for military service in Germany, which left Father with concerns of his own.

In 1938, Ferdinand was now nine years old and Herta seven. Herta was kept from going to school due to the state of unrest in the village. The children at school began to play war, although they had never played such games before. Polish students, once their friends, became antagonistic and waited after school to fight. Older boys bullied the younger ones without adult intervention. Threats were circulated that if a German was caught by the Poles, they would cut their skin and rub salt in their wounds until they would cry out in pain. By this time the girls could no longer attend school, and though Ferdinand had not forgotten his childhood companion Erna, it would be years before he would see her again.

The 1938 school season had ended and the harvest was about to begin. Due to the scarcity of manpower, the village children were now required to do their part to help in the harvest. Emil accompanied them. It was a blessing to the family that he was still with them.

In the latter part of August 1939, the townspeople began tallying all the German families among them. Soon thereafter, all men of German nationality 15 years of age and older, were rounded up by the Polish army and the police. Emil Golke was among them. Due to the heavy population of German families in Volhynia, those taken hostage numbered in the hundreds. The captives were marched under armed guard for several days, without stopping for food or water. Unknown to the captives, Germany and Poland were at odds and German nationals residing in Poland were considered the enemy. Rumors indicated the captives would be taken to a remote location somewhere in the North to be executed.

A few days into the journey, planes flew low overhead. They passed over once and turned around in the distance. Again they flew low over the marching group. The sound of gunfire could be heard in the distance. The sight of the planes returning frightened the captors into abandoning the captives. Hostages and captors alike scattered into the fields in every direction.

A few days before Emil arrived home, the dogs howled continuously as if by some eerie notion they detected something was amiss. After Emil's arrival home, the dogs stopped howling. From that time on when the dogs howled, the family knew there was impending danger. At any time of the night when the dogs began to howl, the family quickly and quietly arose from their beds and hid in the field. Soon thereafter they would see strangers milling about in the moonlight. The dogs were never wrong. They often stayed in the field until dawn, returning only when they were certain it was safe, in order to tend to the cattle and horses.

Our Ukrainian neighbors who were not yet threatened by the political dilemma, were sympathetic and would allow us to hide in their barns and fields so that no harm would come to us. If they suspected anything was amiss, they would warn us. The friendship soon grew thin when even the Ukrainians became fearful of the harm that would come to them if they were found hiding Germans.

Before the fall harvest was finished in 1939, all of Poland was in the grip of terror. Rumors circulated about uprisings and beatings taking place throughout Poland. Many lost their lives during these uprisings.

Political unrest escalates in 1938 and continues in 1939.

Stalin's Polish Policy: In August of 1939, a nonaggression pact between Germany and the Soviet Union was signed, whereas they agreed to split Poland between them and Germany agreed to recognize the Baltic States and Finland to be in the Soviet Sphere, where they would be left alone. This handshake agreement gave Hitler a free hand against Poland without interference from Russia.

Chapter Four

Germany Invades Poland

In September 1939, the Blitzkrieg or lightning war brought about the surrender of Poland. Soon thereafter, land entitlement was abolished, private property and industry was nationalized, and collective farming was instituted. It also left behind a campaign against Polish landowners with revenge attacks, torture, and the murder of many Poles. Soon thereafter, a half million Reich Germans were settled in the territories annexed from Poland. # 829 "Hitler and Stalin by Allan Bullock, McClelland & Stewart Inc. Toronto On.

The "Exchange" Would Soon Begin

In September 1939, the invasion of Poland began in the early morning hours. It was sudden and unexpected and caught the Polish National Guard asleep in their beds. The "Blitzkrieg" or "lightning takeover" was swift and deadly. Within six weeks, Poland surrendered.

A new land policy. Under Stalin's control, land entitlements were revoked throughout Poland. It is said that Stalin believed, "If a man is allowed to own his own property, he no longer works for the good of the masses." Under Stalin's order, industry became the property of the state and compulsory labor was introduced which included everyone from the age of 14 to 60. The insatiable demand to supply the war was a large burden on the people. Drastic measures were taken in order to maintain control.

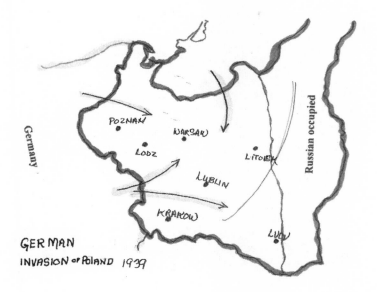

The End of Our Village Life

After generations of deprivation in Prussia, the German immigrants had come to Poland with the promise of free land
and future prosperity. It appeared as though the dream of a
better life would soon come to an end. Volhynia, Ferdinand's
birthplace, and the place that he had grown to love had now
disappeared from the map. New borders were established,
drawn up between the two superpowers. Even with the borders now being defined, that was not the end of the ethnic
strife, and it had not brought the peace that was promised.
The Poles were incensed and began to get organized through
the underground. Rebellion was eminent.

Chapter Five

Exchange—Lost in a Detainee Camp

1939-40

In December of 1939, three months after the "lightning war," and during an extremely cold winter, the "Exchange" began and continued throughout January 1940. This process was designed to relocate people according to their nationality, in order to establish stronger national ties.

> *There were reported to be over 400,000 ethnic Germans in the annexed territories of Poland. Most of them were re-settled in the district of Warthegau during the "Exchange," and as many as 350,000 ethnic Germans who had settled in Russia along the Black Sea coast fled Russia in advance and was included in the resettlement. The Volksdeutche, or ethnic Germans, brought in from the province of Volhynia and the half million Reich Germans, or Germans born in Germany, were given land annexed from Poland. (Hitler and Stalin by Allan Bullock ... McClelland & Stewart Inc. Toronto ON.)*

The "Exchange" required the uprooting and relocating of a whole population of people. Under threat and in fear of their lives, the colonized people had to leave their homes and all of their belongings to be relocated somewhere in the West. Although history suggests that it was a failure, there was one thing that did happen; it disrupted the lives of millions of people for many years to come. At this time, the children living in Volhynia were removed from their parents and sent by railcars west to a detainee camp near the border of Germany.

There was never a satisfactory explanation given as to why the children were removed and not allowed to travel with their parents. The only logical reason for doing so might be that it would ensure compliance to the order and to force (for) the cooperation of the villagers. In fear of losing their children, many families picked up what they could carry and began fleeing to the North and West. The Golke family would be among them.

As each family vacated their homes, Russian replacements waited on the sideline to take possession of them, along with any remaining livestock that the Volhynians had left behind. For the Russians, the takeover seemed a heavenly reward. The resettlement for them seemed like coming into the "Promised Land." They had come from the northern parts of Russia and had lived in relative poverty. For the families like us, having to give up our homes and possessions, the story was notably different.

After the evacuation order, the quiet village of Jachimufka was in total disarray. The "Exchange" was getting underway and the children, now separated from their parents were given a tag to identify them, in preparation for their journey. The tag displayed their names and where they were being sent. The promise of being reunited at a later date helped steady the anxious parents. The children were forbidden to remove these tags and were told their lives depended on it. No one uttered a sound in protest.

At the Golke home, Emil Golke showed deep concern about the family separation but kept it to himself. Emma protested but felt powerless.

Mother delayed us as long as she could in order to sew money into the lining of my clothes. She made me promise not to tell anyone about the money and she said it was to be used only for survival. By this time I had no real idea just what only for survival meant, but I would soon find out.

Only minutes before the train departed, Mother tearfully helped us aboard. We were the last to board the crowded railcar before the door was closed. Mother's final request to me was to keep the younger ones at my side and not to let go of each other's hands.

The three Golke children, Ferdinand ten, Herta eight, and Frieda four, were now aboard the train leaving their home for somewhere unknown. Due to an oversight, they were without identity tags pinned to their clothing. Without them, it would be some time before they would be discovered or reunited with their parents. Ferdinand would soon overcome the feelings of abandonment that had overwhelmed him as the train began to move. He was reluctant to shed a tear. His only concern for the future was to keep his siblings safe from harm.

There was standing room only in the open-air railcars designed for shipping cattle. Benches had been hastily constructed around the edges of the cattle cars, but there was not enough room to sit down. It was cold that year late in December and they huddled together to keep warm. The large cracks in the walls exposed snowy terrain as it passed. There were no sanitary facilities and no heat. After a couple of hours into the journey, the air in the railcar was stifling. The train traveled late into the night and the exhausted people were forced to sleep in a squatting position. They began leaning against each other.

I had no recollection of the passing of time, nor do I remember how many days it took to reach our destination. My final thoughts before I drifted off to sleep

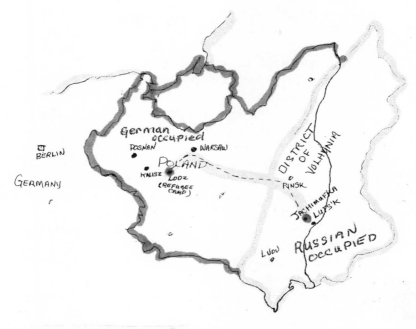

Village of Jachimufka
1929 ~ 1939

Evacuation to
Refugee Camp at Lodz
Winter of 1939

were questions about how our parents would ever find us again.

I awoke from time to time changing my uncomfortable position and attempting to find a new source of warmth from the frosty air. We had traveled for some distance and even in the crowded condition of the railcar; we could see our breath in the cold night air. During the night, people pressed firmly against us. Frieda, who at four years old, was one of the youngest and smallest of the passengers, was crammed firmly against the side of the cattle car by the sleeping passengers. No one noticed her where she lay trapped against the wall barely breathing. After what seemed like an eternity, the train came to a stop.

The doors to the boxcar opened and the cold air rushed in to replace the stench of the boxcar. The elderly passengers needed assistance to disembark. The children were pushed, shoved, and some sustained injuries, but none of them cried. When it came time for us to leave the boxcar, Frieda would not wake up. Her face and lips were blue. I don't know how long she had been like that before anyone had tried to rouse her. I feared that she had died.

People barked angrily at us, "Leave her, she is dead." They said, "Someone will come to take her!"

I refused to abandon her. I repeated again and again, "I cannot leave her. My mother gave me strict orders to stay with her." I said this while the others pushed past us to exit the train.

I felt helpless, not knowing what I should do next. I remembered when Herta had broken her arm and I had laid her in the cradle and rocked her. I wondered if God knew of my dilemma and where he might be right now. I would take her with us and keep her somehow. I picked up her limp body, held her over my head and shook her. As I shook her, to my surprise and joy, Frieda began to breathe! The blue in her face turned pink again, and even though she had not yet opened her eyes, I was overjoyed to know she was still alive.

My arms ached as I carried Frieda for what seemed like forever before we reached the warehouse, located near the city of Lodz, or Licmanstad in German. This detainment camp would become our temporary home. The building was a large brick building, three stories high, once used by the Polish military. I was relieved to finally be able to lay Frieda down in the straw that covered the floor. She had not yet opened her eyes. She appeared to be sleeping and I felt there was no reason to wake her."

At one end of the lower floor of the building, iron stoves held large kettles and the scent of cooking filtered in the evening air. The older women congregated near the large kettles that contained clear broth for the evening meal. No one had eaten since they had left Volhynia, and by this time, everyone welcomed a warm meal. As the crowd began to get organized, the people formed lines and each took their turn filing past the soup kettles for a cup of thin broth. This would be the custom twice daily from then on.

Frieda did not wake up until the morning of our second day at camp. She was conscious but was too sick to eat. She had come down with diarrhea and messed up all her clothes. No one came to help us with Frieda, and it was apparent that if we were to survive this ordeal, we must do so on our own."

Herta and Ferdinand took turns washing Frieda's soiled clothes and then dressed her in them again. They shared their cup of thin broth with her until she began to ask for food on her own. They continued the vigil until Frieda began to show signs of recovery. It was a miracle that Frieda finally recovered. Many of the children died. The winter was cold and many had no one to comfort them.

Lost in a Detainee Camp

Weeks came and went and the three children remained in the camp while others were being moved out. The three Golke children wondered how long it would be before it would be their turn to leave the camp. The bitter winter and the extended separation began to take its toll on everyone. They all huddled together during the cold days and nights in the unheated warehouse. Some blankets were handed out, but there were never enough to go around. Some children went without when the people stole them during the night.

While in camp we could see the city of Lodz in the distance, but we were under strict orders to stay close to the building and never go there. Bad things were happening in the city, they would say. We felt wretched as we had been there some time and had not bathed or changed our clothes. Until now the money that Mother had sewn in my clothes and placed between the linings of my shoes had remained untouched. I remembered that she had said to use it only for survival. We were hungry most of the time now, and the rations no longer seemed adequate. I would have to disobey the camp matron if I were to buy food in the city, even at the risk of being beaten. I was too hungry to be fearful of what could be happening there.

Shortly after the morning ration was served, Ferdinand quickly ventured beyond the camp gate. Without looking back he ran along the path to the road that led to the city. He ran as fast as he could go. When he was certain that no one had followed him, he slowed to a fast walking pace. As he entered the city gates he saw no immediate clue as to the bad things that had been reported to them. He looked around at the quiet city streets and became entranced at the new things he saw there. The tall buildings and the shops that lined the streets were a sight he had never seen before. The buildings had large glass windows, but most of them were broken or boarded up. There were guards with uniforms patrolling the city, but no one prohibited him from venturing there.

I saw sidewalks; some paved and some made of wood. In Jachimufka there had been no such things. I completely lost track of time. I had temporarily forgotten what I had come for, until the familiar pangs of hunger came over me. It was then that I began looking for a place to buy food. It seemed like hours had passed before I spotted a small shop that sold buns and sausage, the kind that Mother had made back home. I peered through the dusty glass and noticed a man inside. As I entered the shop, the shopkeeper stared at me through narrowed eyes. I was sure he would send me out, because he would be suspicious of a child in a store like this. Many children roamed the streets in those days and all of them were hungry. Most of them were very good at stealing food if they were allowed in the shops.

Before the shopkeeper had a chance to send me away, I pulled the threads that held the money Mother had sewn in my cuffs, and his eyes grew large. I handed him the money and asked for buns and sausage, and he gave me a generous portion. I carefully hid the food in the lining of my coat and turned to go.

The shopkeeper's stare followed Ferdinand as he left the store with his booty. In the days to come he would return there again and again until all the money was spent. After taking note of the location, Ferdinand continued to make his way back to the camp; his first real meal on the forefront of his mind. Back in the camp, the three children gathered in a circle, sat down in a quiet corner, and began to eat.

For some time they sustained themselves with the bread and sausage from the daily trips to Lodz. People were hungry in the camp, as the rations were barely enough to keep one alive. At first no one noticed as the three children ate in the corner of the warehouse.

As time went on many began to notice our routine and gathered around to see what we were eating. I am sure that they thought we had stolen the food, but no one made the accusation. It would have been an easy task to take the food from us, but no one made any attempt to do so.

The money soon ran out, but the Golke children had to stay in the camp for a number of months. By early spring most of the children had been reunited with their families, but the Golke children had boarded the train without tags to identify them making it difficult to be reunited with their parents. Those left in camp would be moved to a new camp that was closer to the city of Lodz. The second camp was some distance from the first.

We walked to the new location and the wind was still bitter cold. We had to line up and stay in groups while we walked. Herta's hands got so cold that she began to cry. When we reached the new area, some of the older women soaked Herta's hands in cold water to remove the frost from her fingers.

Without heat in the building where they slept, the Golke children thought the cold winter would never end. They were disoriented, traumatized, and unaware of the passing of time. The children had survived even though they had never anticipated such an appalling ordeal. During the time they were in camp the children grew up quickly, found comfort in each other, and showed maturity beyond their years. Since it was evident that their parents had not been located, Herta and Ferdinand began to act more like parents than children. They took charge of Frieda, who thankfully, never left their side.

I do not remember my eleventh birthday in the spring of 1940. It had come and gone without acknowledgement, as one day was exactly like another. The children in the camp huddled together in groups in order to keep each other warm. To entertain ourselves, we pretended to be back at home sitting down to eat. Pretending helped us cope with the long period of separation and helped us to stay connected to family life.

At the new camp those remaining were becoming very feeble. Some of the children and the elderly were sick. No one bathed or saw to the children's safety. The people suffered from hunger and neglect, but no one complained. Apart from Frieda's illness soon after their arrival, the Golke children had not become sick. Remarkably they were not the worst off of those who remained in camp. They had all survived the ordeal thus far and had remained together.

Chapter Six

Surprise in Erfurt

Lists were posted daily in the camp. These lists named families who were looking for other family members. Ferdinand checked the lists each day but could make out only the requests that had been written in Polish. Even though they were still in Poland, they were considered to be in German territory, and parts of the lists were written in German. Ferdinand could not make out what was written in German. After some time, the Red Cross became involved in finding the parents of lost children. The delay that enabled Emma to sew the money into Ferdinand's clothes had served its purpose, but this compassionate act had prevented them from receiving their identity tags. Now without the tags there was little chance of them being reunited. The Golke children would have to wait a little while longer.

> I lost track of time while in camp and did not know how long we had been there. By now I was sure it had been years, although realistically, I think it was no more than six or eight months. We were there long enough to see summer grow into fall and winter come again, and we would be moved again. I was ten years of age when we left our parents that winter day in 1939, and I do not remember my eleventh birthday which would have been in May of the following year.

At the age of eleven, Ferdinand thought of himself more as an adult than as a child. Taking on the role of a parent had made him grow up far too soon. The carefree life he had known as a child was gone forever, and only a fantasy of it remained. Life in a refugee camp had developed in him a sense of fearlessness and independence. There would be no going back now, except for in his dreams at night, when he revisited the family home in Volhynia and engaged in the childhood games they used to play. Each time he returned he remembered Erna, and he knew in his heart that he had not forgotten her.

Finally one day in late fall, Ferdinand was summoned to the makeshift office in the warehouse where the children resided. He was told that their parents had been located in Erfurt Germany and were residing in a temporary shelter waiting to be assigned. They had frantically searched for the children's whereabouts but to no avail. They finally contacted the Red Cross for help. This final act produced results.

What a joy it was when finally it was our turn to leave the camp. The word we were leaving came none too soon. By this time we were beginning to feel the effects of starvation. It took several days to travel by train from Lodz, Poland to Erfurt, Turingin, West Germany, but I have no recollection of the journey.

Surprise in Erfurt

Upon their arrival in Erfurt, Emil and Emma met the children with a teary reunion. Both Mother and Father acknowledged that Ferdinand had done his job well. To the children's surprise a new baby brother, Erich, was born the end of May 1940, in Erfurt, West Germany. Erich was a welcome addition to the family and almost a year old already. The baby stole the attention of all in the next few weeks as the children took part in his care. Content to be in the company of their parents again, the children adjusted well to their new life and never gave further thought to the separation.

There are some blank pages in my story. I never knew how our parents had arrived in Erfurt, East Germany. They never spoke to us of their experiences during our absence and I admit that I never asked about them. I learned as a child to live happily in the moment and not to ask too many questions. There was much to capture my attention here in Erfurt. Our family enjoyed our time together and the past now was no longer important, as things would be different from now on. The joy of our reunion replaced the trials of our journey, with only one exception. Our parents enjoyed hearing the tales of my trips into Lodz to spend the money they had given us. In hearing the stories, Mother felt in some small way she had helped in our safekeeping and helped to ensure our safe return.

The group home that housed immigrant families was warm and had electric light and running water. The shelter was crowded and the living arrangements were shared among other families, but life was good. For as long as they would remain there, food and other necessities would be supplied.

Everyone in the camp spoke the German language and the children adjusted well to their new surroundings, while the family awaited a permanent assignment. The men in the camp passed the time by congregating at the camp gate to glean any news of the war and resettlement. According to history, the resettlement began in 1940 and continued into 1941. The displaced families were to be assigned homes that compensated for those that had been confiscated in 1939.

Fearing years of uncertainty, the Golkes hoped to be re-settled in Germany under the "Exchange Agreement." The family waited patiently, dreaming of the day when they would have a home again. Germany was being settled rapidly and the Golkes had not yet been called. Emil was apprehensive about the delay and feared that something could still go wrong.

The war was still going on and territory seized in the west of Poland was beginning to be resettled. The newly acquired territory was referred to as New Germany. The uprooted Poles were shipped to the East to a "protectorate" along the Russian border in order to make room for the displaced German colonists.

Father instinctively knew when things weren't going to turn out right. It wasn't long before we found out that his hunch was correct. Our assignment finally came.

Even though New Germany held out promise of a better life, the Golke family found little solace in being assigned there. To them being assigned to Shatenvaulde, in Warthegau, Poland, simply meant they would be returning to Poland, the land they had left behind. These were Hitler's orders and no one could disobey them without consequence. Emma was without words to describe her disappointment. For a number of days the Golkes were filled with regret.

The climate in northwestern Poland was cold and the land was rugged. To endure the necessary hardships and to survive there would be a challenge. It seemed that they had been poorly compensated for what they had given up in Volhynia. Emma knew she had to be strong even with the intensity of her disappointment. With no choice in the matter, and with very little optimism the family packed up and prepared to return to Poland.

Chapter Seven

Resettlement in New Germany

In 1941, the transport to the East began. 400,000 ethnic Germans were resettled in the annexed territories of Poland. The majority were settled in Warthegau. (Hitler & Stalin by Allan Bullock, McClelland & Stewart Inc. Toronto ON.)

1941-42

Upon their arrival in Shatenvaulde, Poland, the Golke's found it difficult to tell which buildings housed the animals and which held the people. The home that the Golke family was assigned was a poorly constructed shack, with a small portion of land and some livestock near the village. Being weary from their travels and finally having a place to rest, the family found no comfort in the place they would now call home. The small stove in the one room shack was still warm indicating that the former occupants had not been gone long and that they must have had a hurried departure.

The newcomers slowly made their way around the farm, discovering what had been left that they could salvage or make use of in the future. The livestock in the barn needed to be fed and watered which gave the family an immediate sense of responsibility. They busied themselves about the farm, providing a temporary distraction from the disappointment they felt. They would leave this place when the time was right, but for now they had nowhere else to go. They knew in their hearts that their flight was not over. Mother began to lament that they had not considered emigrating to Canada as her uncle's, Ernest and Julius Breitkreutz had done, or even to Argentina, as members of Emil's family had done at the turn of the century.

Uncle Ernest, a family man with eight children had shown the most compassion for family members by sponsoring many to live Canada. Ernest had gone to British Columbia and begun a prosperous fruit-growing operation. To write a letter to her beloved uncle Ernest would be Emma's first priority.

Spring had come and the Golke family seemed to prosper in spite of the obstacles. Germany had made a promise to build new homes for the settlers, even though the Golkes harbored no hope of having one. Surprisingly the home inspection declared their home to be the poorest in the area and their name was placed first on the list. Considering the number of homes to be built that summer, the builders tackled the task with lightning speed. The houses were a basic structure and all were the same design. The new homes were simple frame buildings that were a story and a half in height, sturdily built but lacking any nonessential items.

The wooden frame, plaster walls, windows and doors, even the tile roof captivated Ferdinand as he watched the builders from a distance. Ferdinand learned much more than he could have dreamed of that summer. Watching and observing the construction stirred in him a desire to become a builder himself someday, perhaps even an architect.

I was spellbound as I watched from a distance. I rose early in the morning and stayed until after dark, watching and observing until I was sure I could build the house myself. We moved into the house as the last nail was driven into the timbers. Herta, ten, settled in as Mother's helper, and before long she was chastising

Father for entering the house without removing his shoes.
He obediently returned to the door and removed them.

The next three years would go by fast as the family adjusted to village life again. Summer was over and the children began returning to school. Herta was also enrolled in
school for the first time. Emma, lacking a formal education
herself, insisted that girls go to school. As a first time student, Herta was a willing participant.

The strict values upheld by the school administration
were similar to what Ferdinand had known before. Having to
switch the curriculum to the German language set Ferdinand
back for several months. The first week of school the children were tested to determine what grade level they would
be placed in. Ferdinand wrote much of his test in Polish and
was disheartened to learn that until he learned to read and
write in German, he would be placed in the lower grades.

I was humbled to know that Herta, two years my junior,
would start in the same grade as I would. During the next

several years I advanced and became obsessed with getting good grades, even though I received no praise in doing so. Schooling was considered secondary to the duties that were needed at home. Gerhard, who I had known in Volhynia, became my constant companion. We studied together and advanced quickly. The first year we skipped four grades. The following year we skipped two more.

The Bartering Experience in Posnan

In 1943, bartering was still an acceptable unit of exchange. Needless to say no one had money during the war. Villagers preferred bartering over the use of printed money, which from past experience had not been trustworthy.

Ferdinand grew tall in the three years that he lived in Shatenvaulde. Since he was now fourteen, Ferdinand had to be prepared to fill his father's shoes in case he was called to the military. There was still a great deal to be learned. The war was still going on around them, and the conscription was foremost on his father's mind, even though farmers were the last men to be called.

One day Mother suggested that I was growing too fast and needed new clothes. She preferred that Father accompany me to the city, but Father was preoccupied with his work and did not want to leave the farm. At fourteen, I was old enough to go to the city alone.

It was a long way to the city of Posnan and going there was only for the most urgent of reasons. Rumors circulated that it was a dangerous place and political uprisings were reportedly taking place there. This did not deter Ferdinand. He simply could not abandon his yearning for adventure since the day his mother had suggested he needed new clothes. He planned to leave early and return the same day. He would be the head of a family some day and he must be allowed to experience bartering for himself.

Early the next morning he boarded the train to Posnan with his sack filled with produce from the farm; butter, bread, eggs, and honey. There was a shortage of these items in the city and they would command a good price. He arrived in Posnan early in the day. Ferdinand had confidence in his bartering skills since he had learned the art from his father who was an expert at getting the best deal. He was determined to drive a hard bargain.

Upon his arrival, Ferdinand wandered through the streets mesmerized by the sights and sounds of the city and soon lost track of time. He became captivated by what he saw there. The automobiles were what intrigued him the most. I will buy one for myself someday, he thought, even though he could not think of any practical use for them except for the pleasure of the ride. There was plenty of time to discover the city before he had to return to the station to catch the evening train. The shops lined the main street on both sides. The people on the sidewalk hurried along with frightened expressions on their faces and did not speak as they passed. The shop windows were broken or boarded up. Ferdinand wondered what could have happened to break the glass windows.

It was getting late and suddenly Ferdinand remembered the train would be leaving soon, and he had not yet made his purchases. So far he had not located a single shop that sold clothing. He finally spotted a small store at the end of the street. The sign above the door said "Maßgeschneiderte von feinen Kleidung," or tailor of fine garments, but the shop appeared to be closed. The glass was cracked in the storefront window and the blinds were pulled tight to the bottom, in order to prevent anyone from peering in.

Ferdinand tried the front door, but the door was locked. He looked around hoping to find someone to guide him only to discover a man had been watching him. A creepy feeling came over Ferdinand as he wondered how long the stranger had been watching him.

Before Ferdinand uttered a word, the man spoke in a gruff voice, "Go around to the back and knock loudly! They are not allowed to open up!"

Ferdinand did as he was told. He quickly went around to the rear of the building, where he discovered a shabby wooden door. He knocked loudly, but there was no response. He knocked again, even louder than before. Finally the door opened. Through the crack of the door, a slightly-built, middle-aged man with a beard peered through.

"What do you want?" the man demanded.

"I am here to buy clothes," Ferdinand replied.

"Are you coming from the farm?" the man asked, adding, "Do you have anything to exchange?"

"I have goods from the farm," Ferdinand replied.

The door slowly opened. "Come in. Let me see what you have," said the man. His eyes widened hungrily as he looked at the goods that Ferdinand had brought. "Thank God!" the man exclaimed. "I'll take all that you have! Please," he begged, "take anything you want in return."

Ferdinand had expected to drive a hard bargain, but this bartering experience had been easier than he had imagined. He picked out three sets of clothes, a pair of shoes and a cap and resisted the urge to take more. He gathered the items and packed them tightly in the empty sack, thanked the shopkeeper and left in the same manner that he had come.

Ferdinand looked back over his shoulder as the shopkeeper called out, "Please, come back again!"

Ferdinand noticed that the shopkeeper wore a star sewn to his shirt. He stood silently for a moment deep in thought, as he tried to recall where he had seen this symbol before. He remembered only that most of the men with beards wore a star. Perhaps there was a connection, he thought, as he continued on his way.

Pleased with his purchases, Ferdinand held his bag tightly and boarded the train for home. While he sat on the train his mind recalled the experience of the day. He couldn't help thinking that there was an element of fear all around him in the city of Posnan. He couldn't quite make out what it all had meant.

On September 19, 1941, the Jews were required to wear the "star". Yale Univ. Press "Safe Among the Germans"

Chapter Eight

Conscription

The Fall of 1943

In the first three years while living under German occupation, the Golkes experienced relative peace in the village of Shatenvaulde but with very little in the way of prosperity. Had it not been for the home that was built for them, the family would have continued their trek to the West.

There was an element of uncertainty about the state of the war in 1943. Even though farmers were called last, others in the village had already received orders to enlist. The call to military duty still loomed over the household. Emil could still be called.

The men of Polish descent remaining in the village after the Exchange had been exempt from the military. They were assigned to work on the farms as replacements for the farmers who were taken by the military. In this way the farms could continue to produce while the farmers went off to war.

It was not until the summer of 1943 that Emil received his notice to enlist. It was an order that could not be refused. After Emil left for his military assignment, a Polish worker was assigned to the Golke farm. The new farm worker, a man named Grezgorz, proved to be hard-working. Grezgorz was not married and appeared to be approximately 30 years old. He settled in the shack at the back of the big house that the Golke's had abandoned two years before. A few days later a woman arrived to help with the household duties. There was no money to pay these people, but there was food and a place to live.

Emma had no problem communicating with the new arrivals, as she was fluent in the Polish language. They had experienced much of the hardships that the Golke family had undergone, which soon created a bond between them. The Golke family shared what they had and for the time being, they managed well during Emil's absence.

> After a few weeks, Father wrote and also sent pictures taken of him in uniform. He no longer looked like the farmer we had remembered but like a distinguished gentleman in his military finery and highly polished boots. Mother treasured the pictures. Father wrote that he had been stationed in Germany during military training, but he would later be sent to France. Due to his farm experience Father would be assigned to tend the Generals' horses. The Generals were the upper ranks in the military and tending the horses would keep Father from serving on the front lines. Mother was relieved, thinking this might ensure his safe return. Unknown to us, fate had other plans in the works.

News Spread By Word of Mouth

By early 1944, the war was not going well for Germany. An accurate account of the war was difficult to obtain by the common people. The villagers did not trust the wire service and depended mostly on news coming from the underground. All the radios had been confiscated in 1939 and in 1944 people were still fearful of being caught with one. Those who managed to have one in their possession were reluctant to admit they had it. Conflicting propaganda was broadcast throughout the area by means of loud speakers in the villages. It was difficult to sort fact from fiction.

Reports of cruelty and the deplorable treatment of those presumed to be "Feinde des States," or enemies of the state, were discounted as preposterous. The Golkes believed wholeheartedly that they were living in a civilized world where no such things could happen.

In Father's absence, it would be my duty to stay informed, in the event that we would have to flee again. I made trips to Shatenvaulde to gather information about the war. By this time Hitler's army had lost the assault on Moscow, and it was rumored that the Allies had claimed France. Even though I was a mere youth, I knew this would mean Poland would soon be in the center of the war. Fear began to mount among the German-speaking villagers. In the event of war with Russia, it would not be wise for them to be caught in the Russian zone.

For now even though they had no permanent reason to stay, the family would remain in the village in order for Ferdinand to finish his last year in school.

School Ends and Military Life Begins

I was still in school when the Allied forces reclaimed France. We still had no word from Father. It was my last year of school and all the boys that were fifteen were being prepared to enter the military as soon as the school year ended. By this time, most of the families in the area had lost a father, brother, uncle, or a cousin, and we feared that even we might not return from the war. We had dreams of what we would do with our lives after graduating, and none of the boys wanted to go to war. My two closest friends and I, Gerhard Radky and Erich Eschner had received the order to enlist.

Erich's father was a retired military man and a staunch disciplinarian. He had been assigned the job of burgermeister, (spelled in German) or village administrator, when the German occupation began. Since Erich's father managed his household like he did his military assignment, Erich avoided any conflict with him. He spent many hours at our house in order to avoid his father's discipline. Mother welcomed my friends and treated them like family. Both Erich and Gerhard played a large role in my life as we were growing up. We had been closer than brothers throughout our school years.

Though Hitler's recent losses had taken their toll on our morale, our teacher continued to advocate the honor of the military and the obligation of all young men to serve Hitler. He continued with this unyielding conviction right up until the last day of school. In reality, while we were respectful of our teacher, he was not successful in convincing us that serving Hitler was an honorable sacrifice to make. After the school year ended in 1944, our teacher disappeared suddenly and without a word to anyone. Rumors circulated that he fled back to Germany on the last train that left the station that day.

(1944-1945) June 6, 1944, Allied troops landed at Normandy. France was liberated by the Allied forces and Emil Golke was taken prisoner of war. The news of Emil's plight had not reached the Golke family.

Chapter Nine

My Military Assignment

It was the end of June, 1944. I had turned fifteen the month before. It was precisely one year since Father had enlisted, and I would be required to follow in his footsteps.

All of the boys graduating that year received the same order. Gerhard was my best friend and confidant. We made a pact with each other to stay close throughout our lives and remain best friends. We even carved our names in a tree trunk to symbolize our lifelong friendship. We enlisted together on the last day of June, 1944. We had hopes of staying together, but since Gerhard was a year older than I was, he was assigned with Helmut Schindler to the base camp in the north. Erich Eschner and I were assigned to the reserves at Kalisz and remained in training. Erich and I were temporarily exempt from duty on the front lines, but we were afraid that our location at Kalisz was directly in the line of fire. It was located in a basin that was considered a corridor of the war. It was within a few days travel of Berlin, the center of German military might and also the city where Hitler resided.

Erich and I arrived in Kalisz by train late in the day, on the last day of June, 1944. We were given an armband to identify that we were in the army reserves, even though we were not required to sign any official document. We lined up and a photograph of each of us was taken. Erich and I became roommates in the barracks and were rarely out of each other's sight.

It wasn't long after my arrival that I experienced firsthand that life in the military was far different than what I had been led to believe. Our barracks was a highly secure building surrounded by an eight-foot fence and topped with barbed wire to prevent anyone from entering or leaving without permission. Wounded and broken soldiers returning from war were assigned to be our military instructors. The battle scars they displayed did nothing to encourage us that military life was anything more than great personal sacrifice and suffering.

Our daily routine was divided between two exercises. Marching drills and digging endless miles of trenches. We left the barracks early in the morning and marched for hours before we reached the trenches. While we were out in the field, we were allowed to forage for what we could find, but we were not given rations until we finished the day's duties. We were told it was designed to toughen us up, which we would later be grateful for. While in training, we were driven to the point of exhaustion and if we fell short of the Com-

mander's expectations we were told that we would be sent to
the front lines. Each evening, we returned from the trenches
with our boots heavy with clay, looking more like consign-
ees of a penal institution than soldiers.

Every day of the next three months Ferdinand spent beside
his friend Erich. Their friendship helped them heal from the
daily drudgery of the trenches. Digging the trenches seemed
to the enlistees like an exercise in futility.

When their commander was not watching, the two would
talk and plan their future when this nightmare war would
be over, even though with each passing day the war esca-
lated, with no end in sight. Each day as the young men returned to the barracks hungry and exhausted, the security of
the barbed wire fence surrounding the barracks did not offer
them feelings of safety or comfort. The physical demands
and the lack of compassion for the newly enlisted men began
to take its toll on their morale.

By 1944, many German soldiers, growing tired of the war,
abandoned their posts. It was rumored that there were as
many deserters as those being killed at war.

They had come through the end of summer in the trenches.
There was a shortage of uniforms in the military and there
was little hope that the new enlistees would be given warm
clothes. They feared a bitter winter would soon be upon
them. Due to the high incidence of desertion, the movements
of the troops were closely monitored.

It was as though peering eyes were everywhere; as
we slept, when we arose, when we marched, no matter where we were our commanders seemed to know.
We were reported and punished for any slight deviance
from the daily routine. We soon became disheartened
by the extreme demands. The harder our daily tasks
became, the more determined I was to leave and the
perfect time soon would be here. My mind was made

up. For the first time, I felt a new sense of power come over me.

The Plan

Ferdinand gave hours of careful thought to a plan and as of yet, he had not revealed a word to anyone. His mother would visit soon, and he would be entitled to a visitor's pass for the day. It was customary for the military to allow each enlistee a day pass when family would come to visit. This privilege was extended to the newly enlisted as a gesture of moral support for their service in the military. This would be the time when he could move around freely with minimal restrictions. He would be able to put his escape plan in motion.

For a brief moment I had a desire to tell Erich my plan. From the bottom of my heart, I wanted to trust him with my secret but fear of the plan failing stopped me. For now I thought that I would keep it to myself.

While Ferdinand was planning his escape, Emma was at home preparing a small sack of personal effects to take with her, remembering to pack the socks and gloves for Ferdinand that she had painstakingly knitted. A few sweet treats were also added to the sack. By now Emma missed Ferdinand desperately and regretted losing him to the military at such a young age. She longed for the war to be over so both her men could come home again. The train would leave Shatenvaulde early the next morning.

Back at the barracks Erich had observed that Ferdinand seemed oddly withdrawn. Ferdinand told him he was thinking about his mother's planned visit. Erich had spent many days and some nights at the Golke home and had been treated like a member of the family. Ferdinand had not counted on Erich's insistence on visiting Emma with him. This would make things more difficult for him, but Ferdinand did not have the heart to turn him away. It would be a giant leap of faith to trust Erich, even though Ferdinand had no reason to believe his friend would betray him.

Mother arrived and was met at the station. I obtained a visitor's pass for her and led her to the small reception area where we were joined by Erich. After a polite and friendly greeting, Erich sat back quietly in his chair.

Mother expressed joy in seeing both of us and was anxious to learn about our military life. Erich and I looked at each other in unison, as if to decide how much of our military experience we should reveal.

I began to tell Mother the details of our military life even though it was not what she expected. She listened attentively but showed no emotion. I confessed my intent to leave the military in front of Erich, and ironically, he was not surprised. As a rule, Mother was not easily persuaded though she had been my best advocate in the past. This time her longing for my return appeared to have overtaken her fears of consequence. Mother agreed to help carry out the plan.

Since Erich was now privy to all the details, Ferdinand invited him to come along though he did not resort to persuasion. Erich's answer came as a surprise. He hesitated, as if trying to gather his thoughts and then continued, "Ferdinand," he said, "I will not stay here a day without you."

Before the visit was over, the plan went into action. Ferdinand switched his belongings with his mother and carefully hid Emma's bag out of sight. They obtained a pass for Erich so that he too could accompany Emma to the evening train. He was issued the pass without hesitation.

The three of us went to the station together, with my satchel of belongings tightly tucked under Mother's arm. I would return to the train with Mother's belongings before the train left that evening. Even though we had our passes, we would have to return to the barracks in order to be counted at the evening meal. If we were reported missing for the evening meal, it would be no time at all before we would be caught and detained.

Erich and I wasted no time. We sat at our table eating quickly, then returned to the reception area to retrieve Mother's bag where we had carefully hidden it. Using the pretense that Mother had forgotten her satchel, I announced excitedly to the guard at the gate, "Look what I found, Mother has forgotten her belongings. I must try and return them to her."

The guard opened the gate. "Go quickly!" he said, "The train will soon leave the station. You have no time to lose."

We ran as fast as we could, with our hearts pounding in our chests. We could hear the whistle of the train in the distance, signaling that its departure was eminent. We arrived out of breath to find Mother standing in the stairwell of the coach, waving anxiously. The train began to move as we passed the second bag to Mother and waved goodbye on the station platform. We watched as the train picked up speed and finally disappeared from sight.

We were careful not to arouse suspicion while we attempted to kill time until the sun went down. We would continue our plans but only under the cover of darkness. We avoided contact with the station guard by entering the lighted station. We had our passes in our hands in the event that they would be inspected.

I made conversation with the ticket master. Erich let me do the talking, while he stood motionless at my side. I inquired as to the schedule for the next train to Warsaw. I didn't care about Warsaw, but in case the stationmaster was questioned, he might remember our intent to travel there.

We could see the setting sun framed by the large two storey windows of the station. The platform was empty now and before long our journey would begin. As darkness fell, we crept from the station without being seen and followed the tracks for a number of yards. After reaching the underbrush, we began to run. We ran for at least a mile before we stopped to catch our breath. The first hour passed before either of us spoke. After going quite a distance we heard the next train coming toward us. As it rumbled down the tracks toward us, we prepared to jump aboard the train. When the caboose was in sight we hurried to catch a grip at the rear of the car. We both had scrapes and bruises from the experience but managed to make it to the safety of the deck. We lay back with a sigh of relief as we looked up to see the stars shining brightly in the sky.

We traveled for several hours before the train began to slow down, a telltale sign that the next station would be coming into view. We jumped off the train at a safe distance and crept past the station in the underbrush. It was just as we had suspected. There were guards at the station inspecting each passenger. Had they suspected that we were missing so soon? Our passes would only have run out at midnight, only an hour ago. As the train left the station, we jumped aboard again and continued our journey, arriving at home at approximately 5:00 a.m. the following morning.

Mother was relieved to see us but concerned at what trouble we might be in. Erich expressed his fear knowing his father would punish him. He had planned on joining relatives in Canada after he was out of the military, and he decided there would be no better time to do that than now. We said our goodbyes with the intent of seeing each other again. The thought never occurred to me that I was seeing my friend Erich for the last time.

We fell into bed but woke early that morning. Mother had not slept well and expressed concern that the authorities might be looking for me. At 8:00 a.m. sharp, just three hours after my arrival at home, the military police were at our door. I wondered how they had found me so soon. I offered no resistance when I was taken into custody. I was taken to the police station for interrogation. I became consumed with how I was going to get out of the trouble that I was in. During the interrogation the officer demanded to know the reason why I had deserted my military post. Having no real reason to give,

I remained silent. I thought of Erich's father who had been the village burgermeister. Perhaps he could intercede on my behalf. Then I wondered if he had sent the military police to my door so early that day. I knew I would have to handle this myself. There would be no one there to plead my case. The interrogator, a German officer himself, surely would relate to what I had to say.

The officer demanded again, "Why did you abandon your military post?"

This time I boldly spoke in my own defense. "I was treated like a slave. I was subjected to hard labor, starved, and not given warm clothes. Is that how you treat your comrades?" I asked him boldly. "What would you have done if you were treated like that?" I continued, "After all, I am a German too!" I said to him with brazen boldness.

It was obvious that I had gained no sympathy as the officer, while appearing surprised by my outburst, made no attempt to reply. I was taken into the next room where I was told that they had no choice but to charge me with desertion and reminded me that if convicted the penalty would be death by firing squad. My court date was set. I would face a military tribunal on January 6, 1945.

Desertion was considered to be treason against Germany, carrying with it the penalty of death. Cold chills went down my spine. Even though the charge was far more severe than I had anticipated, I could not bear the thought of returning to the barracks. I was released and told to go home to my mother. I was surprised that I had been let go. Surely they knew that I would escape again before the fateful day would arrive. Perhaps the commander had anticipated that I may have that in mind and had sympathy for me after all.

Mother's face was ashen by the time I arrived home that day. She was having second thoughts as to whether she had made the right decision to enable me in my escape. In the following days, I began to think seriously about what I had done. At first I reasoned that at the age of fifteen, there could hardly be a conviction. I changed my mind after hearing of others who had fallen into their hands. I could clearly see that I might be executed before my sixteenth birthday. From that day forward, I was consumed with indecision about what to do about my trial.

We had come through the first year without Father, and to leave now meant that Mother and the three younger children would have to make it on their own. A harsh winter had set in and it would be impossible for the family to escape to the West until the spring of the year. I couldn't risk waiting that long.

I thought it was unfortunate that I had not gone to Canada with Erich. It was only then that I realized that the military police had never asked me about Erich. This seemed highly unusual to me at the time.

Chapter Ten

Escape from Certain Doom—Bridge to Freedom

The year 1945 was the most eventful year of my life. There was not a day that passed that did not carry with it some significant event. Due to those events I would have to have an angel on my shoulder in order to survive. The next eight chapters reflect the events of that tumultuous year.

Escape from Certain Doom

It was nearing the end of December 1944. Ferdinand was at home awaiting his trial and growing more anxious with each passing day. A terrible winter storm had set in that delayed him from leaving in order to escape prosecution. Each day that passed brought added apprehension. January 6, 1945, the date of Ferdinand's prosecution was fast approaching. It was the peak of the war and the Germans did not take kindly to deserters. Ferdinand knew that a conviction would be inevitable and it would end in death by firing squad. As the fateful day grew closer, he wondered about the location of his friend Erich, who had fled with him from the barracks. He began to regret that they had parted and had doubts that Erich could make it to Canada on his own. Ferdinand's mother paced the cabin floor anxiously watching for a sign that the storm would end.

She began to speak with concern, "Father may not return, but I can't bear the thought of losing you also, Ferdinand." She said, "I have prepared some food and extra clothes. I filled a sack with hard-tack and dried fruit to keep you from starving. You must leave soon. The guard could arrive to get you at any time. The children and I will join you as soon as we are able."

It was the first day of January when the storm finally broke. The heavy snow had stopped, but the bitter cold remained. I stepped out of the cabin into the cold morning to pile wood near the entrance of our cabin. The snow crunched beneath my feet. Before long the frost had penetrated my ragged gloves and was nipping at my hands. I returned to the house to get warm when without warning, a man burst through the door of the cabin. His appearance was frightful and his uniform was tattered and torn. He was covered in snow and chunks of ice had frozen to his unshaven beard.

Mother asked the man his name, but for the moment he was unable to speak. Mother sat him in a chair by the fire and gave him something to eat. He ate ravenously as though he had not eaten in a number of days. It did not take long for the ice to melt from his beard and the heat of the stove to revive the man. It was only then that we recognized him. He was a neighbor we had known from our village in Volhynia. We were overjoyed to see him, but the tale he told was frightening. We had no idea that the Russians were so close to us.

Wolfgang had been engaged in battle with Russian troops a few miles to the north. He had been heavily involved in combat and had lost his platoon. When the battle was over he felt his chances of survival were grim. Wolfgang believed that he had been the only survivor of his platoon. As he lay breathless on the cold ground along with the others, he knew it would not be long before they would find him and discover that he was still alive. He clutched his bayonet tightly in anticipation of one last stand. The storm raged around him, and the cold nipped at his body where he lay among the others. It would not be long before the enemy would discover him. He felt the end of his life was near.

He waited and watched as (while) the Russian army began to tally their success from the battle. The wind began to swirl around him where he lay motionless on the ground. Daylight slipped into evening and the cold wind howled around his head. The blowing snow left only shadows of the remaining scene. Wolfgang rose to his knees and crawled quietly away through the cover of the swirling snow.

Wolfgang was on the run now and terrified. He asked Mother if she could give him some of Father's clothes. He hurriedly changed and deposited the tattered uniform in the fire.

"This war with Russia is a bitter war. They will kill me if they find me here," he said. "They are only a few miles away and they are raping and killing everyone in their path. You are a German, Emma," he said. "Your life is in danger. You must leave this place if you value your life."

He grabbed the loaf Mother packed him for his journey, thanked her for her kindness and fled in the same hurried manner that he had come. His departing warning was as stern as he could muster. "Leave now!" he urged. "Your lives are in danger, they will take no prisoners! There is no time to lose!"

Mother and I looked at each other in dismay as our friend disappeared from sight. Up until now we were ignorant of any impending battle, but there was no doubt that the news of the Russian advance was factual.

I forgot my own concerns and began to fear for Mother and the children. We had to come up with a plan. Mother suggested that we all leave together since the storm had now subsided. It was only three days travel to the West where we would be safe. The eastern border of Germany was heavily guarded, but the Russians would not go beyond the Oder River. We would be welcomed and given sanctuary in Germany if we were fleeing from the Russians.

It was bitterly cold that early January morning, but the sun shone brightly. We got ready for the journey by wrapping our shoes with straw and tying them with cords to keep our feet from the frost. Mother carefully placed some treasured keepsakes in a sack and packed only what provisions we could carry. Mother needed help with the wagon since it had become bogged down with heavy snow. She suggested that we ask Grezgorz to lend a hand. Grezgorz was standing by the barn and had been watching us for some time without offering to lend a hand.

Mother explained to Grezgorz what we had learned and then asked him if he would like to come along with us. He was reluctant to answer at first, but then he suggested that he would come with us as far as the main road. It was clear that he had no plans to leave Poland. It appeared that even the loyalty of our friend Grezgorz had become painfully thin. When he spoke, he spoke convincingly of a Russian victory. While he wished no real harm to come to us, he was hopeful that the Poles would be liberated by the upcoming battle. He had his heart set on the return of his home and property.

Grezgorz would stay and take part in the "jubilation." Perhaps for a moment, Mother had forgotten that the war would be different for Greg than it would be for us. Perhaps our Polish friend knew more than he had told us. Our only solace was that we had treated Grezgorz well during the time he resided with us. In return for our good will, he dutifully removed the snow from the wagon to help us be on our way.

It was the very next day, the second day of January 1945, when we made our hurried departure. War with the Russians was looming and my inevitable court-martial was only days away.

I took the reins as Grezgorz jumped from the wagon when we approached the main road. "This is as far as I can go," he said.

As we continued along the road, there was not a soul in sight. It was disconcerting to believe that danger really existed in such a peaceful setting. The silence of the morning, the sound of the horses as they snorted away the frosty air, and the absence of anyone on the road at this hour made the scene surreal. Could we have been mistaken about the urgency? We wondered if we had been the only ones who knew of the danger looming on the horizon. Our thoughts again drifted back to the day before and to our friend Wolfgang. Surely he had not been mistaken.

After traveling several hours in this serene setting, some of the fear that had consumed us the previous day had now subsided. Mother had grave concerns that began to occupy her thoughts. These concerns were evident by the expression on her face. Her sister and her family as well as her father and brother remained in the village. Fearing that Mother was having second thoughts, I urged her to continue. It would be unthinkable to turn back now.

We would be safe only beyond the Oder River. In the back of my mind I could think only of my conviction and death by firing squad and the Russian army not far behind.

"Maybe we should have warned the village," Mother lamented.

It was becoming apparent that Mother's heart was not in the journey. Just as we had done five years earlier, we were leaving all we owned behind and our future was unknown. Fleeing had never been easy, and it had always been in the wintertime. We had experienced bitter cold and hunger each time, and this time would be no different. I was more certain than the rest that we would make it to safety if we made it to the bridge. I had to keep reminding Mother of this in order to keep her spirits up. I drove the horses hard along the snow-covered road. A team of horses could travel 200 kilometers in a period of three days. That was the distance to the bridge and safety. In three days time we would reach the bridge over the Oder River. From that time on we could leave our fears of doom behind us.

Before long, we could see the form of a wagon approaching us in the distance. We could make out the silhouettes of at least two men riding on the wagon. We were not sure if they were friend or foe. Surely the Russians would not approach us from this direction, we thought, but who else could be on the road this early. I kept my composure and held tightly to the reins as the wagon got closer.

Now in full view, we could see the men on the wagon were the burgermeister, or mayor and an associate from Shatenvaulde. The two appeared quite pious in their worn and tattered German uniforms, with their bayonets at their side. They had been given the job of overseeing the village of Shatenvaulde at the beginning of the occupation and they took their job seriously. They were returning to the village and were not aware of an encounter with the Russians. They hailed us and approached our wagon.

"Where are you going?" the men asked.

We told them the news we had received just the day before. They looked at each other in surprise. The two men stepped from the wagon and spoke to each other out of earshot from us. They appeared to be in disbelief. After pondering the information we had given them, they eventually spoke.

"If this were true," they said, "the people in the village should prepare to leave. We should all go together, as there is safety in numbers. Come back to the village and we can all go together. We will butcher a pig and pack provisions," they said convincingly.

"Returning now is simply preposterous!" I shouted.

A conflict arose between Mother and me. I wanted to keep going, but Mother wanted to return to the village.

"No!" I protested, "We must not return to the village. Can't they leave without us?" I asked. "We will reach safety over the Oder River if we keep going now!" I insisted.

Mother had been thinking of those who had been left behind and was convinced that it was best to return to the village and join the others.

When Mother made up her mind that was that! I had been taught to be respectful, but I knew this time that Mother was wrong. Regardless, I turned the wagon around and returned to the village, with the burgermeister following directly behind.

It took the remaining men one whole day to organize the troop. It took another day to prepare the horses and load the wagons. Many of the women and children were without husbands and fathers. Conscription and tragedy had drained the village of manpower. I worked as hard as I had ever worked in my life thus far. It was now almost three days since we had returned to the village. Only two days remained before my court-martial. How could Mother have made this mistake?

"We cannot wait one more day for them, even if we have to leave by ourselves," I urged Mother.

Finally, late into the third day, we began our journey out of the village. The wagon train was more than two miles in length. As we went along the road many more joined the troop. The wagon train was so large and conspicuous that we felt like sitting ducks. Most of the people fleeing were German. If we encountered Russian troops on the road, we would be defenseless. The only ones with guns were the village elders and it would be crazy to think that they would be able to defend all the wagons.

For awhile nothing seemed to go right. It was bitterly cold and we were going at a snail's pace as one malady after another occurred. The first day we were plagued by wagons breaking down, and there were no spare parts to repair them. We were forced to let some of the horses loose from the broken-down wagons and abandon them, while other wagons tried to accommodate the less fortunate. The remaining horses had to be fed and watered. Some of the horses just refused to go any further.

"Now we are even at the mercy of these stubborn horses!" I protested to Mother. "If only we had kept going!"

Another day into our journey and we were ordered off the road to allow a battalion of German troops to pass. The military had first priority on the road. We lined the side of the road as they sped by. The troops would not stop for anything, much less our convoy of horses and wagons. The number of trucks carrying troops and soldiers numbered in the hundreds. If this was Hitler's army, they were wasting no time. The army came from the Oder river bridge and was headed in the direction of our village. We were more determined than ever to press on. Only one more day and we would reach safety. Our friend from Volhynia had been right all along.

Bridge to Freedom

We arrived at the Oder river bridge early the next day, January 6, the very day that I was to be tried for treason. Already I began to feel relief. Our family was the third wagon to approach the bridge. The two wagons ahead had already ascended, with a safe distance between them. The rushing water of the swift-flowing Oder River had not yet frozen over, in spite of the cold. I took one last look behind me and contemplated for a moment about all we had left behind. In the distance I saw a fleet of blackbirds flying in the billowing clouds, while the sun shone brightly in the early morning sky. There would be no court-martial now and the fear of death by firing squad was fading from my mind.

Chapter Eleven

Trapped in the Russian Zone

The first two wagons had ascended onto the fragile bridge over the Oder River. The Golke wagon would be the next in line. Ferdinand and Emma waited their turn. The wagon ahead of them had to be a safe distance away before they could advance onto the bridge. Ferdinand could hardly wait for their turn as he gripped the reigns. Within minutes they would be over the bridge and safely on German soil. Even the horses seemed to be impatient as they waited to begin their ascent onto the bridge.

I looked again at the blackbirds that seemed to be getting larger as they approached us. Before long we could see that I had been mistaken. The specks in the sky were not blackbirds at all but planes that were fast approaching. It was too late to turn around now. It appeared that we were right in the line of fire with no place to run.

The Russian planes flew low over the waiting wagons and soon they were beside us. We could see the pilot's faces as they bombed the bridge. The blast was so forceful that the fish from the river became embedded in the cement pillars of the bridge. The horses and wagons and the people that had been on the bridge floated past us in the swift-flowing river. It sickened us to see the sight of it. The Oder river bridge, our bridge to freedom and our only means of escape was now reduced to rubble. We were now *trapped in the Russian zone!*

There was panic among the villagers as they anticipated the return of the planes. Some abandoned their wagons and attempted to flee on foot. Others attempted to turn their wagons around. Some wagons got stuck which prevented others from turning around. Mass pandemonium set in, and for several minutes no one knew what to do. To return would mean facing the enemy head-on, but to stay would be impossible.

The officials of the village were consumed with fear. Their former bravado had turned to melted butter, and their legs were visibly shaking. They came to our wagon, with their heads in their hands.

"What can we do now?" they begged to know.

I was so angry that I couldn't speak. I was completely dismayed that they had made us turn back on our first trip. I thought that listening to their foolishness might have cost us our lives. The men began to weep.

Mother finally convinced me to speak to them, though I wondered why they would turn to me for any advice. After all I was one of the youngest of the men and had no military experience except for digging trenches. I did however, have a knack for getting myself out of trouble. Suddenly I had an idea!

"The first thing you are going to do is to get rid of those uniforms and your guns!" I told them. "Any indication that you are military will get us all killed! Throw the guns and the uniforms down the well!"

They did as I told them while people collected articles of clothing for them to wear. We then began to plan our next move. We decided we had to turn the wagons around which took most of the day. We agreed to go back in the direction that we had come, two at a time, putting distance between each wagon. Perhaps this might ensure that some of us would survive. From now on, we would take one day at a time.

The first night we settled in an abandoned house and barns that we found along the way. We fed and watered the horses and found a place to lay down to rest. We continued back in the same direction the next day, and we passed the place where we were forced off the road by the military.

A mile further the scene began to change. It looked like there had been an ambush. From this point on, and for several miles, there were dead and frozen bodies of soldiers lying on the side of the road. Mother covered the eyes of the younger children as we passed. The German army had sustained heavy losses. Perhaps this was all that was left of the troops that had passed us on the road. We headed back in the direction of the farm in Warthegau, where at least we would find shelter from the winter cold. Back at home we would be better equipped for survival.

We arrived back at the house early in the evening of the following day and found Grezgorz was nowhere to be seen. A layer of new fallen snow covered the ground and masked the ugliness of the day. We gathered some kindling to make a fire and took up residence in the shack at the back of the big house. Judging from the deplorable condition that the shack was left in, it was certain that Grezgorz had no housekeeping skills. It was worse than it had been when the Poles had left for the East. Even so we would stay there since Mother was certain we would be safer there. She said that if the Russians should come, they would go to the big house first.

Mother lit the fire and began to burn the pictures of Father in uniform and the letters she had treasured along with anything that might indicate that we were German. We couldn't chance lighting the fire again. Smoke coming from the chimney would give away our presence. We were sure that it would be just a few days before the Russians would be among us. If we were to remain safe, we must be thought of as Poles. An eerie silence prevailed as we lay down to sleep that night, as the last vestiges of warmth from the fire disappeared.

RUSSIAN ADVANCE TO BORDER
    OF POLAND AND GERMANY JAN. 1945.

Chapter Twelve

Russians Arrive at the Big House

Less than a week passed until the Russians arrived. You could smell them from a distance because of liquor and poor hygiene, and just as Mother had predicted, they began to occupy the "big house" which was closer to the road. We hid in the barns behind the big house and stole into the drafty shack to sleep long after darkness had fallen. Throughout the long winter days, we watched the Russian soldiers come and go. It was hard for us to see the soldiers help themselves to the winter wood that we had piled near the rear entrance of the house while we huddled together in the cold.

So far the intruders appeared not to have noticed our presence, or other matters of greater importance took their attention, we did not know for sure. We had to remember to speak Polish from now on. Perhaps the soldiers would think we were harmless peasants, which in reality that was what we were. We might be shot without mercy if they thought we were German.

The Russians were now patrolling the road, and there was no doubt that we were under Russian occupation. For the time being, we remained in hiding and for the next several days, we did what we could to tend the livestock in the barn without being seen. We did not leave our shelter until after dark. The Russians had not checked the barn yet, but we expected they would do so soon.

Encounter on the Road

We had no news from the village after we returned to the farm and we hungered for news of any kind. I began to slip away occasionally without being seen and then returned quickly so Mother would not be alarmed. I spied on the soldiers as they went about their daily regimen. I knew I would be in peril if I were to have an encounter with them. I became braver each time that I felt I had outwitted them.

I finally told Mother I would try to make it to the village. I was confident I could cross the road without being seen. Mother was nervous at my suggestion, but needless to say, there was no holding me back. I carefully took note of the soldiers' positions while I remained in hiding. They were staggered at a distance of approximately fifty feet from each other. I held my breath as they passed just within yards of me while I hid out of sight. I counted the soldiers as they went by, and I was sure that I had seen the last of them when I ventured onto the road. I was mistaken, as I was now within the range of another soldier. Immediately I knew that it was foolhardy of me to think that I could outwit them.

"Останвить!" ("Stop!"), the soldier yelled out in Russian as he raised his rifle, pointing it directly at me. I stopped dead in my tracks. The soldier called out in Russian, "я буду стрелять Вам сейчас." ("I'm going to shoot you now!")

I uttered a silent prayer, *"God in heaven, please help me!"* Just then someone called out his name and for a brief moment the soldier turned his head. My prayer had been answered, and in a split second I was gone. I ran back through the thicket as fast as I could go, back in the direction that I had come.

The soldier again raised his rifle, and since he had been cheated out of his kill, he took aim and shot a dog that had crossed the road ahead of him. Satisfied now, as if he had accomplished what he had been expected to do, the soldiers resumed their marching, each about fifty feet apart.

I finally reached the shack where we lived and burst through the door out of breath from my run. Mother was

clearly upset with me after learning of my encounter. Days went by before she would allow me out of her sight.

The younger children got tired of staying in hiding. No one had approached us so far, even though we were quite sure that the Russians knew we were there. We gradually lost some of our fear, and Mother allowed the two younger children to play outside with the order to stay out of sight of the big house.

One day while on her way to the barn with a pail of water for the horses, Mother was confronted by a Russian soldier who had been watching her. He spoke to her, but Mother had no knowledge of the language. He repeated his request again with gestures. Mother realized he was asking her if she had any liquor. We knew the Russians had a reputation of tanking up on liquor, which often gave them the courage to do any sort of deed.

Mother did her best to communicate that we had no liquor. Convinced that she had told him the truth, the man turned back toward the big house and left us alone. That evening by the sound of the revelry coming from the big house, it was clear that the soldiers had managed to find some liquor on their own. We stayed far away from them.

Later on the soldiers confirmed that they were more comfortable with our presence when they asked Mother to bake them some bread and tend to their horses. She did her best to do what they asked, while staying at a safe distance. Since the Russians knew we were there, there was no need to huddle in the cold any longer and Mother began to light the fire.

Working in Forced Labor

After the Russian occupation of Poland in early January, the first priority of the military was to bring the large Russian trains as close to the border of Germany as they could. The train rails had to be moved eight inches to the left to accommodate the wider wheel base of the large Russian trains. By this time Russia had claimed territory as far west as the western border of Poland. The conquest of Germany would soon follow.

Late January and Early February 1945

The incoming flow of Russian troops had slowed down in Shatenvaulde and community life was returning. New statesmen were assigned to the village under the command of the Russians. Property ownership was abolished and forced labor was instituted. Anyone fifteen years old or older, was rounded up to work in forced labor on the rail line. My limited knowledge of the Russian language made me an asset to the Russians as an interpreter for our labor group. Using me as an interpreter worked well when I was asked to relay their commands, but it annoyed them when they discovered I understood their private conversations. I hoped they had not discovered that I had learned of their intent to penetrate Germany before the end of the year. They were trying to keep some things top secret. At that time it was early in February, and the end of the year was far away.

Under forced labor we worked from dawn to dusk with small rations. We were guarded by armed Russian soldiers the entire time. At the end of each day every man was counted. It was during the labor on the rail tracks that I learned of the brutality of the Russian soldiers firsthand. They bragged of their escapades, each attempting to outdo the other while they sipped on their ever present-flask of Vodka. I initially dismissed their bragging as "whiskey talk" until I experienced the sting of their brutality for myself.

The guards would beat any person who was not strong enough to drive the large iron peg into the wooden railway ties in three strikes of the mallet. I had been given several lashes of the whip, even though I had tried hard to accomplish the difficult task. As the day went on the men had all grown tired. We stopped only when we were told to stop and were given food only at the end of the day.

It was painful for me to watch the guards use their whips on the weary men time after time. One day, motivated by the sting of the whip, I became too bold for my own good. Impulsively I spoke up to the soldier in charge, without consideration of his rank or position.

"Why did you whip me for this?" I asked, and, "Why do you punish these hard-working men?"

I realized too late that I would probably be shot for my insubordination. Instead, the Russian officer took a match from his pocket, struck the match and threw it to the ground.

He turned to me and said, "This is all you are worth! You are absolutely nothing!" He continued, "I can't waste the bullet it would take to kill you for your insolence."

I am sure the need for manpower was the only thing that saved my life that day. I did not know it at the time, but my actions that day had gotten the attention of the Russian high command. All I knew then was that I would avoid a confrontation from then on.

It had been several weeks since we began, and we had moved many miles of track. I was hoping to be discharged soon. It was late in February 1945, or possibly the first of March when we finished the job on the rail. Since one day was the same as another, it was hard to keep accurate records of the passing of days. The Russian trains could now reach the German border with ease, and it was accomplished far ahead of schedule.

Chapter Thirteen

Return of the Angry Poles

It was early in February 1945. I was working in forced labor on the rails and had no knowledge of what was taking place at home with Mother and the children when the following occurred.

Back at home the Russian soldiers were still occupying the big house, and Mother had been approached to tend the horses. She went about her business and kept the children at a safe distance from the soldiers, when one day she was faced with a big surprise. The Poles who had been forced to leave their farm, arrived back to reclaim their home and possessions in a foul frame of mind coupled with resentment. They were angered that the farm had changed in their absence.

Mother feared admitting how long we had been there would bring consequences so she pretended ignorance. She did not let on that the big house now occupied by the Russians had been built for us. Survival was her main concern, and she would need time to think of her next move. Even though the new arrivals barked out orders and obscenities in the Polish language, as if somehow Mother shared the blame for their misery, she treated them with kindness. They asked her what had happened to the barrels of dry goods* and the

---

*We had discovered the booty of goods soon after we arrived. They had been buried in such haste that they were easily found. Assuming ownership, we took the dry goods and kegs of honey to the market in order to barter for other much needed staples. It would not be wise to admit any guilt now.

pails of honey that they had so carefully buried before they were forced to leave. Mother pretended not to know.

The Russians had not yet vacated the big house when the Poles arrived. When they reclaimed the shack they once called home, which Emma and the children now occupied, the barn was the only place left for Emma and the children. Ferdinand had not returned from the forced labor camp and there was nowhere else to go. Emma gathered what little she had left and claimed a quiet place in the corner of the drafty barn. She felt her only option was to work hard to please the Poles so she could remain there until Ferdinand returned. For a few weeks, all went well.

Celebration and Suffering

The Russians soon vacated the farm for a more suitable location in the village. The first task after they left was to clean up the house, as the soldiers had left it in a deplorable condition. There was human feces in every room. It took days of laborious work before it was fit to inhabit. Emma and Herta joined the Poles in the clean up.

After the Poles moved into the house, Mother moved back into the shack. The Poles began to prepare for the jubilation. They began to make whiskey from the grain and to bake cakes from the flour that the Golke family had made the year before. They took the large iron kettles that were once used to boil mash for the cattle to begin the distilling process. After many years of rugged use, the kettles were not suited for distilling and the fire was stoked far too hot.

As Mother passed the red-hot kettles, one of the lids blew off, which made its contents explode. The scalding mixture covered Mother's entire abdomen. Her bloodcurdling screams could be heard for a distance. The force of the explosion was so strong that the door blew open and the children, Eric and Frieda, who were playing in the yard, were splattered across their face and arms. The agony that followed was indescribable.

Lacking much empathy for Emma who lay near death on her cot, the Poles continued to prepare for the long-awaited jubilation. Ferdinand never knew how long Emma laid in agony before he arrived home from working on the rails.

Earlier on the Rail Tracks

February was over and we were well into the month of March. I was getting tired of the laborious work and hoped I would soon be discharged. With the workers from the north now in full view, the end was in sight. By midday the tracks would meet and the job would be completed. I was among the last of the troops that were discharged that day. For days now, while working in the cold, I had felt an uncanny sense of urgency. My thoughts kept drifting back to home and family and I hoped all was well. The sun shone brightly in the sky as I left for home that day. In looking back at the miles of tracks that had given us so much anguish, I recalled a scripture I had once read, "The sun shines equally on the righteous and the wicked." My spirits lifted as I headed in the direction of home.

I imagined I was at least ten miles from home as I walked long into the night. The air was crisp as frost gathered around my mouth and nose. In the distance the dogs barked. The sun was up long before I spotted our home in the distance. The smoke from the chimneys of both houses rose straight up in the cold of the early morning sky. The scene gave me both comfort as well as a sense of alarm. What could account for both of the fires burning? I knew Mother had not made a fire in the shack before I left. I began to feel a tinge of panic.

My arrival was nothing like I had expected. Mother lay in pain on her cot with only a light fabric covering her body. I was shocked at the extent of her injuries. The burns were so deep that her skin hung without being attached. I felt a sense of helplessness. "How could Mother survive this? I feared that she would die. I hung my head in my hands and prayed, "Oh God, what can I do now!" Impulsively, I ran out into the yard where a deposit of clean clay lay in a mound. I gathered the clay, moistened it into a thin pliable compound, and gently covered Mother's abdomen with the thin paste. She expressed immediate relief.

I could think of nothing else but the fear of losing Mother. I had to get her to a doctor! "She can't die like this!" I begged prayerfully.

There were no doctors in the village and there was no horse or buggy to be found. The Russians had taken them all, and the Poles had nothing to offer since they had gone through hard times of their own. There was no question about it, I was on my own. I prayed that Mother would not be taken from us. I would have to go for help in the village. There might be one last hope to find a horse and buggy, I thought. There was someone in the village I had to see.

I ran the whole way into the village, and went straight to the newly appointed village master. I told him about Mother's tragic accident and asked him to loan me a horse and buggy. His reply was firm.

"That is impossible!" he said. "There is no horse and wagon in the village!"

I turned to him and in desperation, I insisted angrily, "You must get me a horse and wagon or I will go to the Russian military police and report what you are allowing in the village!"

I really knew nothing of what could be happening in the village that would incriminate the man and apart from motivating him to help me, I could think of no reason for him to be afraid. Perhaps his reaction alone had given him away. I wondered what had turned his face so pale and what he feared that would change his mind so quickly.

"Wait here, and don't move from this spot," he said as he quickly left the house. He soon returned with a horse and wagon. "I risked my life for this," he said as he handed me the reins. "Take it and don't ever come back here," he said angrily. "I don't ever want to see you again."

I grabbed some straw and lined the bottom of the wagon and then gently placed Mother onto the straw. I covered her to keep her warm. Even though I had no idea where I was taking her, I instinctively headed in the direction of another village a few miles down the road. I was certain there would be a chance to find a doctor there.

Russian Field Hospital

I traveled for about an hour before I saw signs of a community in the distance. Mother had stopped groaning, and I thought she may have drifted off to sleep. I was still unsure of where I was taking her and looked for anyone who I could ask. There was a man piling blocks of wood near a house along the side of the road. I stopped to ask if there were any medical facilities close by. He looked startled when I spoke to him in Polish. He motioned for me to keep going in the same direction.

"There is a field hospital up ahead that treats wounded soldiers. Ask someone there," he said.

We arrived at the makeshift hospital. I spoke to the attendant in Russian. "Is there anyone who could see my mother," I begged. "She is badly burned."

The attendants followed me to the wagon. When they removed the blanket that covered Mother's wound they gasped in horror. One attendant upon seeing her condition placed his hands on his head and exclaimed, "Oh My God!"

As we carried Mother into the clinic she groaned in pain. They couldn't give her anything for the pain as they cut away the skin that hung from her abdomen and cleaned the clay from her wounds. They applied a medicinal salve gently on the open flesh and carefully placed a thin piece of gauze over it to seal the wound. They gave me extra bandages and told me to keep the wound clean and dry.

"That is all we can do!" they said as they motioned for us to go. I thanked them again and again for their help as I turned the wagon to return in the direction we had come.

In a matter of days Mother was beginning to show signs of improvement. Even so, it would be some time before she could move from her cot. I tended her wounds each day, and with Herta's help, we managed the chores. Herta was invaluable during the next several days since she never left my side.

The new landlords complained constantly, because Mother could no longer do any work. I was certain we would have to move again. I immediately applied in the village for a new place to stay, hoping we would be able to stay together. It would not be easy to find a place for a family of five that only had one worker. I would try and make up for the others by working hard for the Poles as long as they allowed us to stay. For several days we remained in the shack on the farm.

Chapter Fourteen

Living Under Russian Occupation

Those who remained in the village settled into a routine that required total compliance to the newly established order. Since we had been in Poland since birth, it was not difficult to convince the Russians that we were Polish. Most of the villagers began to lose their fear of the Russians, but it would be a mistake to trust them completely.

Mother had improved greatly but had not recovered fully from her burns. We had not yet found a new residence when I had to go into the village one day leaving Mother, Herta, and the children alone in the shack. During my absence, and without warning, a group of Russian soldiers entered the door of our shack. They asked for money and liquor. Mother replied that she did not have any. When she did not rise from the cot, a soldier walked over to her and tore back the covering that hid her bare wounds. They were not a pretty sight even though in reality they were healing well.

Not knowing what they were seeing, the soldiers gasped and backed away in horror. They left Mother alone in order to search the pantry, which was the usual place to hide money. They found none. Some of the men who appeared unsatisfied to abort their mission entirely, began to stare at Herta as she cowered in fear behind Mother. Herta was thirteen years old but looked younger than her years.

"Leave her, she is just a child!" the leader of the crew barked. They left the shack and did not return. For some time after this happened, Herta stayed out of sight.

The attitude of the Poles had not changed, and we knew we had to leave soon, so I inquired daily about a new place for us to stay. We were finally assigned to a Polish farm on the other side of the village. The new place was larger than we were used to. The farmers name was Lukasz. His greeting was stern and unfriendly when we arrived, and from the beginning it was clear that the family would only be able to stay for a short while. Something told me that I would not like this man. His appearance was unusually large in spite of the fact that food was scarce through the war years. I began to think of him as the "fat farmer" although I kept my thoughts to myself. Mother and the children could stay on the Lukasz farm only until the Russians decided what to do with her.

It did not take long for Lukasz to put me to work, and even though it was unbearably cold and Mother had not yet fully recovered from her wounds, she was not offered any comforts. She and the children were to stay in the barn and keep out of sight.

I finished my chores early one day and thought I should waste no time in returning to the farm. I arrived just in time to see that Lukasz had been enjoying some sport. Erich, my younger brother, then five years old, was trapped inside the fence where a billy goat was kept. Lukasz and his cronies lined the fence and roared with laughter as the goat bunted Erich to the ground. No one made any attempt to rescue the terrified boy from the goats repeated attacks.

The laughing stopped when the men began to notice my early arrival. For a brief moment the men glared at me as if to say, "If you know what is good for you, don't even think of interfering." The momentary distraction of my unexpected arrival gave Mother enough time to remove Erich from inside the gate. He was tear-drenched and terrorized from the experience. Erich clung to Mother as she comforted him, and from that day on he stayed by her side.

It wasn't long before Mother and the children were taken to a house in the village. It had been abandoned and was now being made available for the orphans and elderly. I was confident that Mother and the children would be safe there. Sympathetic individuals donated food and clothes which were distributed among the residents. News of Mother's plight traveled throughout the villages, and soon an herbal salve arrived at her door with instructions about its usage. It had been handed down from village to village until it arrived. Mother applied the salve to her wounds and immediately found relief from each application. The salve helped the wound to heal, and flesh and skin began to grow over the wound.

The family settled in and Herta began to work in the village. Mother worried about Herta, fearing for her safety. The soldiers had a reputation for debauchery, but that was not the only fear. Polish-speaking deviants also contributed to the anarchy simply because no one stopped them. On one occasion Herta was walking along the street with a young Polish friend when a Russian soldier cornered the two of them. The soldier took out a picture of a holocaust which he carried in his pocket.

The soldier said to Herta, "This is what you Germans are doing, what do you have to say about that?"

Herta had never seen anything like this before and did not reply. The soldier let her go but later told her Polish friend that he would have shot Herta on the spot if she had said one word in defense of the Germans. Miraculously no harm came to her.

The demands of the Lukasz farm kept me from visiting my family for some time. I looked forward to the end of winter and longed to feel warm again. The manger where I slept behind the horses was covered by empty grain sacks and was my only shelter from the cold winter. I remained on the fat farmer's farm through the month of March while I prepared for the new planting season.

Chapter Fifteen

Top Secret Mission

By April 1945, Hitler withdrew troops from the east along the border of Poland because of heavy demands for more troops in the South. By April 20, 1945, Zhukov's and Koniev's forces from Russia were inside the Berlin city limits. Brackets are ours. (Hitler & Stalin by Allan Bullock, McClelland & Stewart Inc. Toronto ON.)

My sixteenth birthday was less than six weeks away, and it was because of that that I am able to remember with certainty the precise time and date of my top secret mission into Germany. I was looking forward to my birthday in May since turning sixteen was considered a significant event in a young man's life. If we had been back home in Volhynia, there would have been a celebration to mark the event. It held little significance now in the midst of turmoil, but the dreams of those times kept me from despair.

For a number of days now I had been preparing for the spring planting on Lukasz's farm. I turned in early one evening after a gentle rain had fallen. Early the next morning I was suddenly awakened by a commotion outside the barn. The village reeve had come to fetch me. This was the very same man that had told me he never wanted to see my face again.

"Come quickly," he ordered. "The commander has sent for you. They want you for a mission of great urgency. They will shoot you if you refuse," he added. "Don't tell anyone about their request."

The apparent urgency of the matter sent chills down my spine. I could not think of any reason why I had been chosen for a matter of such importance. I went along with him immediately.

As they entered the village square, soldiers were visible on every corner and a military presence dominated the village. Ferdinand was led into an interior room of the building that now housed the Russian headquarters. He was led into a well-lit room. He wondered what could be so urgent. The answer was not long in coming.

The Russian commander who stood before me was no stranger. He was the very man who had whipped me on the rail tracks and told me I was worthless. Now he required a favor? I could barely comprehend the idea. I did not like the man, but I remained respectful.

The rank of the soldier was much higher than I had anticipated. I realized now he was one of the Russian high command. He began to speak in Russian since he remembered that I understood the language.

"You have been summoned for a top secret mission," he said. "You were chosen because you speak the German language well, and as I remember you have a fearless nature. If you refuse to do this job you will be shot!" He said this without flinching. "You will be given a horse and wagon to take some passengers into Germany." He continued, "I am waiting for your answer."

I felt a distinct sense of dread come over me. I thought I would be safe for now if I agreed to do as he asked. I was alive today, but I had no guarantee that I would be tomorrow.

The request seemed to be a simple task, and the commander wanted an immediate answer. I wondered why they needed a German just to drive a horse and wagon. Perhaps the soldiers had no talent in managing horses ... I wondered, but I didn't ask any questions. I simply agreed to do as he asked.

I could not imagine the importance of the mission, or what might lie ahead of me in attempting to cross the heavily guarded German border. I was instructed that I would have to speak convincingly to the border police if I were interrogated. They were trusting of course that I would not give them away! The commander told me my duty was to escort his men into Germany. If I were successful they would let me go, and no harm would come to my family.

Germany's decline! By the end of March, 1945, bombers destroyed much of Berlin and Munich. In the West allied forces bridged the Rhine and were driving hard toward Germany's industrial heartland in the Ruhr Valley. In the East the Soviet army was preparing to cross the Oder River, less than 100 kilometers from Berlin. The German people feared that the Russian troops were acting in vengeance for alleged atrocities. ("The Master Plan" by Heather Pringle, Hyperion, New York.)

It was early in April 1945, when I began my first journey into Germany. Six Russian soldiers accompanied me in the wagon. Some of the men were covered by tarps, and one was in the seat beside me. He held his gun hidden by his side. From a distance our wagon appeared to be loaded with peasants from the forced labor camp that was being relocated. It would take careful examination to detect the real cargo that the wagon carried that day.

For several miles the men did not speak, even to each other. A couple of hours into the journey they relaxed their stern demeanor. They spoke in Russian and told me that they liked me and that I was a brave man. They carried food rations and shared them with me throughout the journey. I played along with their jokes, even though I realized they were seasoned soldiers that would be capable of anything if I betrayed them.

The soldiers carried detailed maps of the journey and appeared to be well-informed. I asked them where they were going. At first they would not answer and only repeated that it was "Верхний секрет" or "top secret!" They laughed at the mistakes I made when I attempted to speak Russian. I was sure that my Russian was better than their Polish, but I kept quiet, and drove the team of horses late into the night.

Within a day's journey we were nearing the border of Germany, and the tension began to mount. It was in the early morning hours when we crossed the border into Germany which we did without incident. There was no one on guard and we didn't encounter anyone.

I didn't know why the border had *not* been secured, but I knew by the soldiers' apparent relief that they had expected a battle. I was relieved that there weren't any guards that I would have to try and deceive. Now it was no longer a secret that *the border between Germany and Poland was penetrable.* I then realized I had made it into Germany for the very first time.

It was only after we had crossed the border into Germany that the soldiers told me they were going to Berlin. I had never been to Berlin, and the mission into Germany had no significance for me at that time. We traveled another hour or so beyond the border, before I was ordered to stop the wagon. My heart raced as I imagined that this was likely the end of the line for me. The soldiers began unloading their gear from the wagon. They asked me if I intended to continue into Germany. I told them I had to return to my family.

"Turn the horse around and go back," they said. "We were ordered to shoot you, but in doing so our presence would become known. Go quickly," they said. It was still pitch dark and the noises of the night rang in my ears as I turned the wagon around to return home. The soldiers disappeared into the night. I had no idea what had saved my life that night, but I was grateful to be alive.

As I drove the horse back in the direction that I had come, my thoughts drifted to my mother and my sisters and brother at home. After awhile I became very weary from the journey that had taken us two full days and nights without sleep. I looked forward to falling asleep in my manger bed behind the horses, covering myself with empty grain sacks. I wrapped the harness around the horn of the wagon, and as the horse continued along the road, I drifted off to sleep.

Before long the sun began to come up, and I was surprised to see that there were people on the road. They appeared to be Polish, and I was happy to see that none were in military clothes. I thought perhaps they were people returning from the resettlement. They were definitely intent on escaping from Germany, and they hailed me as I went by. I stopped the wagon and they seemed to be relieved when I spoke to them in Polish.

"Where are you headed?" they asked. I told them I was going to Poland. They asked, "Could we have a ride on your wagon?"

I couldn't see the harm in that, and I longed for company on my return journey. I also wished to hear reliable news from Germany. My fluent Polish did not betray me as my new acquaintances thought of me as one of their countrymen. They spoke of an expected German defeat in the war, and they expressed anger and resentment toward the Germans. After listening to the harrowing tales for a number of hours, I concluded that they had to be hearsay.

It was just before evening when I crossed the same border point that I had come through just hours before. My Polish companions thanked me for my kindness and disappeared in several directions. I headed toward Shatenvaulde to return the horse and wagon. I hoped by doing so I would be relieved of my duties and allowed to return to the farm. When I arrived I was told to report to the commander. I was quickly hustled into a secure room and questioned about the details of the trip. It seemed strange to me that the commander was surprised that I had returned and that I had encountered no resistance crossing the border.

My hopes of being discharged were quickly dashed to pieces. Since I had been successful this time, I was asked to repeat the trip with another group of soldiers. My heart sank as I realized I would not be able to return to the farm and the quiet stable where I found solitude and comfort.

The second trip was similar to the first. When we arrived at the same location as before the soldiers again bade me farewell, and once again I returned to Poland with more passengers that I picked up along the road. After I got back to the village and returned the horse and wagon, I was allowed to rest a whole day before the Russians sent for me again. They wanted me to make a third and final trip.

As I left the village early the next day, the intensity of the mood seemed far stronger than before. I did not trust these men but saw no opportunity to escape. My fears and suspicions were not unfounded. I overheard the men as they talked to each other in muffled undertones. I could only make out that I would be a menace to the operation if I did not return to Poland. The tension heightened as we neared the same area where the others had gotten off the wagon.

"Stop the wagon!" the commander ordered, and I obeyed. "Now step to the back of the wagon and do not move!" he barked out in Polish.

He waited for the men to remove their possessions from the wagon and continue down the road. In the meantime he stood guard to prevent me from escaping. My heart pounded as I dreaded what might happen next. The commander began to speak to me, surprisingly as well in German as he had done in Polish.

"I have orders to shoot you," he said. "I have decided against it after listening to you talk about your concern for your family. If you return immediately to Poland, and tell no one where you have been, I will let you go."

I agreed to do as he ordered and thanked him profusely for his kindness in allowing me to go.

"Go now!" he said, "and tell no one!" Then he followed his troop into the darkness toward Berlin.

It was late in the evening of the following day when I returned to the village square. I was still shaken by the experience of coming so close to death two days before. I was afraid to report to the commander this time since I realized that he had given the order to kill me so I abandoned the horse and wagon in the village square and returned to the fat farmer's farm. I crawled into the manger with its layer of newly spread straw and fell asleep after covering myself with grain sacks.

Early in April 1945

Notations by the Author.
  Bombings by the Allies had begun in the German capital city. By April 20, it was reported that the Russians had penetrated Berlin. Hitler committed suicide soon thereafter. It was not until more than sixty-three years later that Ferdinand, the protagonist of this story, became aware of the significance that these trips into Germany might have had.

Chapter Sixteen

Siberia Selections

Siberia was located in the far northern district of Russia. Many workers were needed there in order to develop the rich mining resources. The severe cold and long winters made it an unpopular place to begin one's life and family. In the beginning only the most deserving criminals were sent there to work in hard labor, and very few of them returned. Later when the demands of war compounded the need for the resources found in Siberia, Russia began to populate the area by force. When the Russians invaded new territory, people were rounded up off the street and sent to Siberia for any minor infraction. Both men and women were forced to go there.

(The potentate of the insert is the man seated on the far left; Victor is his name. He was caught in the Siberia selec-

tions as a child of four. Victor along with his mother was snatched off the street and sent to Siberia without being allowed to inform their family. His mother eventually died in Siberia. Victor grew up and married a local girl and became an interpreter. He taught high school for a number of years in Siberia before new ordinances forced Russia to allow many of the Germans to return to Germany. Victor along with his wife [also in the picture], and his children returned to Germany in 2001.)

The Siberia selections would begin without notice. Ferdinand found himself in peril yet again when he was caught up in all three roundups. He made a narrow escape each time.

(by Ferdinand Golke): "It was nearly impossible to avoid the Siberia roundups as the Russians used the element of surprise. In our area there were three such incidences that I remember. I was caught in all three. The Russians enlisted the Poles in the area to help in the roundup."

The first weeks of April, 1945, had come and gone, and the Russians wasted no time in getting down to business. They began to enlist the Poles to help roundup people from the villages for the next phase of their agenda which was to select people to send to Siberia. People were picked up off the street without provocation and without warning. They were not allowed to return to their families, or even leave word with anyone as to their whereabouts. Those selected were loaded on boxcars without explanation.

I had no prior knowledge of these roundups, and before I realized it, I was caught in the first one. Initially I was not afraid until I learned the purpose of the roundups. I only knew that I should attempt to wriggle myself out of them somehow.

During the first selection I noticed that they were letting younger boys go while they placed the older ones in a boxcar. Seeing the people that were being chosen was enough to alert me that I had to get out of it somehow. I managed to escape by pretending to be much younger than I was. I was let go and was determined not to be caught in another roundup.

No matter how cautious I was, however, I was caught again in the second roundup that took place without warning. There were many informers, and it was rumored that they were sending Germans to Siberia in retribution for atrocities that they had committed. I did not know at the time what that meant. I was taken back to the same area where they were loading the boxcars. This time I had to think fast as I was desperate not to be included in the selection. I watched who they were setting aside, and it appeared to be people that had physical disabilities. When I was a child playing, I had played the part of a cripple very well. Perhaps I could still be convincing. I formed my legs into contortions and feigned walking with great difficulty. The Russians must have believed me, because I was set aside again. I looked around quickly to see if any of my family was among the crowd, and I was thankful to see that they were not.

When I was caught in the third roundup I was sure there would be no escape. I didn't know when this madness would end. Just then I noticed Grezgorz, the man that had been assigned to our farm. He was standing near the commander on the station platform, and for a moment I was overjoyed to see him again. On second glance it appeared as though our former friend was helping in the roundup. I began to wonder if he would be a friend or foe, but I had no other choice now but to trust him. It would just be a few minutes, and I would be loaded aboard the train along with the others and sent to Siberia. I had to take the chance that he would help me. I ran directly to him and begged him to plead with my captors.

"Please, I beg you Grezgorz, ask for my release to you for much needed farm labor. Please Greg, help me," I begged!

Grezgorz was hesitant. It was plain to see that he did not want to get involved, but then he suddenly changed his mind.

"Come with me," he said.

I walked with him to the guard in charge of the operation. Grezgorz asked the guard politely if I could be spared since I was desperately needed at his farm for the upcoming spring planting. The guard smiled at him as though he knew him well, shook his head in dismay, and released me to his custody.

I thanked Grezgorz again and again and quickly left the station. I knew then that the kindness we had shown to him in his time of need had been generously repaid.

I returned to Lukasz's farm. In the coming weeks I would have no idle time. There was still grain to be thrashed, bagged, and loaded onto wagons to take to market. I worked hard under the watchful eye of Lukasz and fell into the manger each evening at dusk. There I returned to the delightful days of my childhood in Volhynia where I was again free in my dreams.

Chapter Seventeen

Brush With the Polish Resistance

Word spread throughout Poland that Hitler had committed suicide in Berlin on May 1, 1945. On May 7th, 1945, came the unconditional surrender of Germany, signed by German navy officials. May 8, 1945, was proclaimed a day of armistice, or ceasefire. On this day Germans could return to Germany and no harm would come to them.

By the end of April 1945, Poland had been liberated. The Occupation had secured a controlled peace. The Polish underground resistance was operational but had not yet mustered up an insurgence. The underground militia had attracted the enlistment of the Polish youth. These were gangs of thugs that secretly organized militant operations bent on a free Poland. They refused to recognize the new government, and they began participating in acts of barbarism that rivaled the Russians. While they were still operating underground these youthful idealists took pride in wreaking havoc and taking pleasure in causing others pain. There was no one to stop them. For weeks stories were circulated about German spies infiltrating the villages. Ferdinand didn't know of any spies.

My brush with the Polish resistance came unexpectedly one day as I crossed the railway tracks returning from working on an adjoining farm.

90

The thugs lay in wait on the trail between the two farms where I frequently passed. No one used the trail except farm workers. Most of them were German, who after a long day of labor used the path for a shortcut. The thugs approached me on the path as I returned home one day. They had clubs in their hands, and I was outnumbered eight to one. I knew there was little chance that I could escape without a beating. They might even kill me.

They surrounded me and began jeering, "So you are a German are you? You have 'Hailed Hitler' have you?" It was considered a crime to "Hail Hitler" in Poland at this time.

I answered, "No I have not Hailed Hitler!"

They continued shouting obscenities in an attempt to goad me into doing battle.

They shouted loudly, "If you 'Hailed Hitler,' now you can 'hail' us! Go and repeat, 'Hail Hitler to each of my friends here, and bow down when you do!'" they ordered.

I knew there would be no way I could defend myself against their numbers so I did what they asked. They had me repeat the homage again and again while a roar of laughter came from the group. I resented what they were doing, since I had been born in Poland too. Perhaps I was more Polish than some of my captors. Little by little my love for this land began to erode into disdain. Surely this was not how God had intended mankind to live, I thought. Finally when they had not been able to goad me into further resistance, they grew tired of their sport. They let me go, cautioning me that I would not get off so easy if they should meet up with me again. I was intent on being more careful next time.

The incident of the following day left me with little doubt that the experience of the previous day was connected.

While I was preparing to go out into the field the next morning I happened to look up. I noticed a group of men carrying bayonets approaching the farm from a short distance away. Since the previous day's experience was fresh in my mind, I was afraid that the young thugs had spitefully re-ported that I had paid homage to Hitler; an offence that was severely punished. My fears were not unfounded.

I did not wait around for their arrival. I ran toward the barn instead seeking refuge. I thought I had not been seen, but soon the men were in hot pursuit. I was sure I could out-run them. After entering the barn I could think of nowhere to hide, so I buried myself beneath a huge stack of hay that cov-ered the barn floor. I waited silently under the hay, terrified to move or breathe for what seemed like an eternity. Then I heard the men enter the barn.

Speaking in Polish they said, "He must have come in here! Now we'll get the German!" My heart sank when they shouted, "He has to be in the hay."

I silently began to pray. The men stabbed their bayonets into the hay with mighty thrusts. I felt the blades pass within inches of my face and body though somehow they did not pierce me. They stabbed into the hay again and again just missing me by a hair.

I held my breath in case the sound of it could betray me. Since they had not been successful in striking me, they seemed convinced that I was not in the hay. They left the barn to search other outbuildings where they thought I might have gone. I stayed under the hay all day until nightfall, afraid that they might still be waiting for me. Lukasz did not even come to see if I was still alive.

The following day when I had fully recovered from the experience, I felt elated that I had escaped once again. The thugs must have been satisfied since there was no further incident. Once again I began my duties around the farm. I continued to work from daylight until dark for Lukasz, but I longed to visit my family. I still had not figured out how to approach Lukasz to ask permission. He rewarded all of my hard work for him by sending me to his brother Jozef's farm with more work to do. I was becoming sick at heart over this place.

Chapter Eighteen

Blind Man in the Barn

When my assigned tasks were done I had to report to Lukasz's brother Jozef. I resented being sent to Jozef's farm initially, but little did I know this would turn out to be a blessing in the end. From the very beginning Jozef acted more like a friend to me than a taskmaster. He was a younger man than Lukasz, a bachelor, and he appeared to be the better of the two.

It was while working on Jozef's farm that I had a memorable experience. After finishing my chores early one afternoon, I noticed a man sitting near the entrance of the barn. When I spoke to the man he returned my greeting. I thought he was German since he spoke to me in that language without an accent. I surmised that he had been hiding there in Jozef's barn. Perhaps he knew I had been coming and going for some time, but this was the first time he made his presence known.

He asked, "Please sir, please, can you give me food, because I am blind. Can you give me food? I have no money or any other means."

Even though I had next to nothing myself, I was moved with compassion for this man. Seeing his dilemma reminded me that there were others worse off than I was. I began to share my rations with him. He ate hungrily and thanked me again and again. Ironically I was happy he was there and looked forward to seeing him each day when I returned from the field. He was someone who needed and trusted me; I knew I could not abandon him. I never told anyone of his presence for fear that harm might come to him.

Each day I looked forward to finishing my work so that I could return to the blind man. One day he asked for a piece of soft wood that he made a small carving from.

"This is all I have to give you in return for your kindness," he said.

Though he never told me he was leaving he suddenly disappeared. I felt a great loss when I returned to the barn to find that he was gone. He had left as mysteriously as he had first arrived. The gratitude he expressed for my kindness had touched me more deeply than I had expected, and my thoughts have returned to him at different times throughout my life.

With all the changes going on around me, I began to grow anxious about my family even though I knew they were not far away. I was confident that Herta would take good care of Mother and would stay close to her. She had always been a willing worker even at a very young age. She had gotten a job in the village working as a housekeeper which took her inside the Russian military headquarters. Herta was paid a small wage and was sometimes allowed to take food back to Mother.

Winter work on the farm was just as laborious as the harvest was in Poland. The grain that had been harvested from the previous year was now thrashed and had to be sacked for the marketplace. If there were extra bags of grain, they had to be carried up a ramp to be stored in the granary. These bags could weigh well over 200 pounds each. Younger workers were chosen for the chore of walking the heavy bags up the ramp. After hours of strenuous work with the bags, I became faint and collapsed. This was the first time that I was aware that I had any limitations.

I recovered from the incident, but the weakness would return from time to time. It had not been long since I began working on the farms in Poland, but I was already longing for a reprieve. When I had a moment to reflect, I remembered that I had once been free. I had dreamed that I would someday lead my family to safety, but I realized now that this was just a dream. My impoverished condition became worse with each passing day. My shoes were soles carved from wood with straw wrapped around my feet and legs to prevent them from being cut on sharp twigs. I slept in the barn behind the horses, covering myself with empty grain sacks to keep me from the winter cold. The rats and mice ran over my face at night, and I was too exhausted to push them away. In the mornings I would stand in the bright sunlight to pinch body lice that snapped between my thumbnails.

There was very little hope of improving my life here in Poland, and because of my circumstances I was destined to remain in hard labor. I began to hate the farm, and I longed for a skill that would rescue me from this daily drudgery. Since Lukasz was a harsh taskmaster and certainly not a generous man, I had no hope of improving my circumstances through hard labor. I made up my mind that someday I must leave Poland.

I had been robbed of my childhood, and I was dreaming an unattainable dream while I wallowed in despair. I lacked self-esteem and a sense of worth. Even my memory of Erna was beginning to fade. My sixteenth birthday had not yet arrived, and already I had reached the lowest point of my life, a life without hope. My heart was broken over everything that had happened in this land. I had reached the pinnacle of despair and was desperate for a change. Silently I made a vow, "If I survive I will never return to the country of my birth and never again speak the language!"

Chapter Nineteen

Escape after Midnight

May 7th, 1945

In two short weeks I would turn sixteen, and I decided I
would see Mother on my birthday no matter what. Perhaps
Jozef would be kind and allow me time to make the trip.
With that goal in mind I worked extra hard to bag the sacks
of grain for him. The grain would go directly to the market. I
dreaded how much work that was still to be done before the
warm spring rains began.

The sun was getting stronger and the days grew longer.
The worst of the winter was over, even though a dusting of
new fallen snow covered the ground. I had finished most of
my work at Jozef's farm. Jozef had gone to the market and
had not yet returned. It had only been a short while that I had
known him, and even though I resented being sent to him at
first, I now wished that I could remain with him. Somehow I
had grown to like him. He was more compassionate than his
brother who appeared to have been hardened by hard times.
As I pondered the differences between Jozef and his brother I
suddenly felt that I knew why the blind man had appeared in
his barn and why he had disappeared so abruptly. Jozef had
hidden fugitives there and had known he was there all along. I
was pleased to realize that my blind friend would still be safe.

I was returning home from Jozef's farm when I met him
on the road. He was returning from the market. He stopped

me and asked me if I felt well that day. I did not answer him immediately since I hoped Jozef had not learned of my collapse. Maybe his concern for me was genuine, and if it was it was more than I had expected of him. I answered him by saying that I had been more tired than usual lately.

He remarked sternly, "Don't let Lukasz get the better of you! He is an impossible man Ferdinand, and he has no love for Germans! He will work you to death if it is left up to him! Perhaps you should leave this place and get out of there. You are no longer safe there!" he exclaimed.

Jozef then asked, "Have you heard of the armistice?"

I replied, "I have heard nothing." Nor did I know what "armistice" meant.

Jozef explained that the armistice was an officially declared cease fire agreement whereby Germans could leave Poland without interference.

"The armistice is to take place tomorrow," he continued. "You could leave Poland and go back to Germany where it will be safe for you," he said. "I am going back to Germany myself someday when the time is right." "If you want to leave you will have to make up your mind quickly," warned Jozef. "The armistice will be for one day only." *(Official Armistice "ceasefire" May 8, 1945.)*

Jozef seemed unusually persuasive about my going back to Germany. I didn't tell him that for me leaving Poland was merely a dream.

Jozef continued, "Why don't you go then?" he asked. "Go back to Germany where it is safe for you!"

I confessed, "I cannot leave without my family, and I have no money for the fare."

Jozef quickly replied, "I will help you! I sold some grain today and you can have the money." He reached into his pocket and pulled out all the money he had gotten for the sale of the grain, and gave it to me. "I was treated well in Germany," he said, "now at least I can pay something back."

I was reluctant to take the money since I did not feel that I had earned it. Jozef insisted that I had worked hard for him and that I should take the money and go. I could hardly contain my gratitude. What could have instigated this fine gesture? Jozef had been more like a brother to me than a taskmaster.

I knew there was no way to repay this man for the generosity he had shown me. I knew only that if I stayed I would die here in Poland, the land I had grown to despise. I accepted his gift with tears in my eyes, and I cannot describe the joy that I felt at that moment! It was as if my prayers had been answered.

I planned to leave the next morning before the sun came up. If I was careful Lukasz would not suspect anything. He would surely prevent me from going, and he would be angry if I left him now before the spring planting began. My life would be in danger so I could not risk a confrontation with him now. I made up my mind that I would be gone before sunrise.

I continued driving the horses toward the Lukasz farm. I was nearly halfway there when I could see a wagon approaching me from the opposite direction. It was dusk and there was usually no one on the road. I hoped that it wasn't Lukasz coming to get me. He had an uncanny hunch when something was going on. I knew that if his brother Jozef knew of the armistice, he would have learned of it too. In that case he would be coming to escort me home and prevent me from leaving.

Sure enough it was just as I had feared, I could see clearly now that it was Lukasz coming toward me. At that very moment I wanted to call him Lucifer. I thought he was more like the devil than a man. My heart pounded as he approached.

Lukasz hailed me, "Where are you going?" he asked.

"I'm coming back with the horse and wagon," I replied.

"Why? Have you finished the work already?"

"Yes we are finished," I said.

By the concerned look on his face there was no doubt Lukasz had something on his mind.

"Then I'll follow you home," he shouted, as he turned his wagon around to follow me.

Lukasz followed closely behind me as we continued in the direction of home, and when we arrived I was afraid of what to do next. I knew that I could not breathe a word to him about my plans. After the brush with the Polish underground I was sure he had a connection with it. I knew what he was capable of. Even his dogs were vicious. To dispel any suspicion I would have to make it seem as though it was a normal day, just like any other.

I busied myself with the final duties of the evening. I fed and watered the horses and returned the harnesses to the hook in the barn. I put the wagon away, washed up, and prepared to retire just like I had done many times before. Lukasz sat near the entrance to the house. His cold stare followed me wherever I went, and I was relieved that he made no attempt to make conversation with me. I continued to go about my business just as though it was any other day. I was afraid of what he would do next since he was not a man that could be ignored for long.

Finally Lukasz broke the silence and began to speak. "You can't fool me," he said. "I know what you are up to. I know you are going back to Germany! Just what do you think you will do there? Be a Policeman?" he scowled and then began to roar with laughter.

I remained silent, not acknowledging that I had heard what he said. I could hardly wait until the time was right when I could leave this place. To stay here now would be unthinkable. Lukasz became silent again and did not get up from where he sat.

Lukasz had never been in the habit of turning from a confrontation. His strange behavior made me wonder if he was actually more afraid that I would leave him, than he was angry. Farm laborers were scarce and I would not be replaced easily, even though he had made threats to replace me many times before. I continued finishing up the chores of the day

and became engrossed in my own thoughts. I silently prepared to bed down in the stable where I had slept many times
before, but this would be the very last time. (*Behind the
horses, in a manger packed with straw.*) As I lay in my bed
of straw I thanked God for my life and the goodness he had
given me that day. I shivered in an attempt to find warmth
and comfort as the night air grew cold around me. At last I
knew that I had found a friend.

An hour or more had passed while I pretended to sleep. I
was certain that Lukasz had not yet learned of his brother's
good deed. By this time darkness had set in, and I was sure
that by now Lukasz himself would be retired for the night or
so I thought. Just then I heard the barn door quietly open. In
the moonlight that streamed through the open door, I could
see the silhouette of Lukasz with his dog leashed by his side.
He stood quietly for a moment looking around the barn. He
stared in the direction of the stable where I was feigning
sleep. Satisfied that I was asleep and all was well he turned
and left the barn closing the door quietly behind him.

I did not move for some time from the manger in the event
that Lukasz returned. I was tired from the day's activity, but
sleep did not come for me that night while I contemplated
my escape. I counted each second that passed as I waited for
the midnight hour.

Escape After Midnight

It would be some time before the sun came up, and by then
I had to be long gone. It was slightly after midnight when
I crept from my straw-packed bed. I stole quietly from the
barn and headed in the direction of the village. I looked back
over my shoulder from time to time not trusting the shadow
that followed me in the moonlight. I prayed that I did not
wake the dogs since nothing escaped their evil eyes. I carefully placed each step I took so as not to make a sound. It
was only after I was quite a distance from the farm that I
finally began to run. The road was empty at this time in the

morning as I made my way toward the village where Mother and the children lived.

I wondered if Mother had heard of the armistice. If she had heard the news she would be expecting my arrival. I was certain she would have everything ready for a hurried departure. There was no way to contact anyone, but I had a strong feeling that I would not be disappointed.

I was nearing the house and became excited to see a lighted lamp in the window as I approached. It was as though a miracle had occurred. I entered the home where Mother lived to find that she had heard of the armistice, and she and the children were ready to leave and had been expecting me.

Mother had no money except for a few coins that Herta had earned from her employment in the village. Assuming that we had no money for the fare, she stopped briefly to devise a plan. When I pulled a fistful of money from my pocket, Mother began to cry. It was a miracle that our plans had come together without a single hitch. Mother hurried us along expressing apprehension that Herta's employer would come to fetch her. By that time she planned to be long gone. We started out along the path through the field before the sun came up. We were hoping not to be seen by anyone before we arrived at the main road. For awhile the weedy underbrush hid us from view. We continued until we reached the road without an incident.

Mother had not yet recovered fully from her injuries, and Erich was too young to walk the distance. It would be a difficult undertaking to make it to Konin on our own. Konin was more than twenty miles away, and it seemed an impossible task to walk the whole way there. It appeared that we had more determination than strength. I silently prayed to God that somehow we would make it safely. As I had experienced in previous times, a new sense of power returned to me.

An hour passed as we walked along the road. I had been carrying my younger brother in my arms. A wagon appeared unexpectedly and stopped beside us. I wondered for a moment if this man was Herta's boss who had come to take her back. In actuality the wagoneer was a man from the village that was making his way to the blacksmith shop to get his horses shoed.

"Are you going to Konin," he asked.

"Yes," we replied.

"Climb in, I'll take you there," he said. "I am going there myself."

I uttered a silent prayer of thanks as we all climbed onto the wagon, and apart from his admission that it was an early hour for young ones to be on the road, the man spoke very little during the two hour journey to Konin.

At the edge of Konin the wagon stopped, and we got out. We thanked the man for his kindness. He bade us goodbye and continued on his way. We walked a short distance to the train station. It was comforting to know that our flight to safety had finally begun again.

Chapter Twenty

Robbers at the Train Station

We were the first to arrive at the Konin station, and to our surprise the ticket master's booth was open. We were able to purchase our tickets right away. As I held my ticket in my hand I began to think that this was the best gift we had ever been given, and I silently thanked Jozef again for the kindness he had shown to me. What he had done would carry us to freedom. Because of the early hour it would be some time before we could board the train so we wandered around the empty building as though we were seasoned travelers loitering about.

It wasn't long before others began to enter the station. Most of the travelers had luggage with them and were surprisingly well dressed. Our travel attire was nothing in comparison. We looked more like Polish peasants who had come from the forced labor camp. This conjecture would not be far from wrong. The people crowded into the station now and scrambled to purchase their tickets. The majority of the travelers spoke German. The temperament of the crowd indicated the overwhelming response to the armistice. There would be many Germans leaving Poland, but many spoke of the fear of retaliation if they did so.

We stayed close together and held on tightly to our tickets. They were the only guarantee that we would leave this place. I vowed that I would never return. We settled together into a corner of the station to wait for the train that would arrive soon. Without warning bandits entered the station platform. They demanded that the passengers give them their luggage, as well as any money and jewelry. After taking everything of value including the people's overcoats, the people had very little left to take with them. We were fortunate to have spent our money for the fare already which left us with no money to be stolen. Strangely the bandits paid no attention to us. Perhaps our impoverished appearance led them to assume that we were poor peasants with nothing of value for them to take.

We began to board the train soon after the robbers had disappeared from sight. We hoped that it would be smooth sailing from now on. We settled together in a booth grateful that so far no harm had come to us. It would take two or perhaps even three days to reach the northeastern border point where we would cross into Germany. The train began to move from the station and Konin gradually slipped into the distance, out of sight.

We watched from the window as we passed fields and villages still covered with a blanket of new fallen snow. There hadn't been any signs for several miles. We were at least a day and a half into our journey when Mother began to worry that something was amiss. She thought that we might be heading in the wrong direction since it was taking longer than she had anticipated and our destination was not yet in sight. We began to wonder if they had deceived us and were taking us to Siberia after all. We checked our ticket stubs to see if something could have gone wrong.

It wasn't long, and the train came to a stop. We strained to see what was happening through the frost-covered windows. More people were boarding the train, and a few moments later it started up again. After about an hour had passed, a ruckus broke out on the train. The robbers from the train station were there and began to rob the people who had just gotten on the train. They took anything they thought was useful including warm coats and furs. It was plain to see that no one would be leaving Poland with anything of value. We were frightened to know the robbers were on the same train as we were. We were afraid of what would happen next.

We had traveled for several miles while all became quiet again. The train had changed direction now, and we could tell by the setting sun that we were headed northwest which now gave Mother a sense of reassurance that we were headed in the right direction.

The Border at Stettin, Poland *(A border city on the Polish side of the border of Poland and East Germany)*

It seemed like forever before we reached Stettin. I had crossed the border with the Russians three times earlier that year, and I was certain there was a closer border point than Stettin. I found out that Stettin had one of the only border points that had rail connections. It was the last border point in Poland before crossing the mouth of the Oder river. We continued northwest for another day. We were getting hungry, because all the rations we had brought with us were gone. We would have to wait to purchase food in Stettin, but no one complained since we had experienced hunger before.

The train slowed down when Stettin came into view, and a sense of great relief came over us. We were scheduled to stop for a short while and then continue into Germany the following day. As the train slowed, we looked out the window and saw people jumping from the moving train. We couldn't understand what was making them jump from the train before it came to a stop. Then we realized they were the very people who had robbed the train. They jumped from the train taking their booty with them. We were happy to see them go and hoped that this would be the last we would see of them. Here in Poland, however, we learned to expect anything.

The city of Stettin was a much bigger city than any on our journey so far. We had expected there would be more assistance for the travelers because the armistice would mean more people were leaving Poland. The one-day cease fire had now passed and assistance for travelers was nonexistent.

We huddled together so that none of us would get separated. We had hoped our departure would be joyful, but it was also plagued with expectation. We had very little money and no food left. We had to melt snow for a meager drink of water.

Our tickets indicated we were to board the train again the next day to cross the Oder river into Germany. There were hundreds of new arrivals as each new train came into the station. Each arrival added to the atmosphere of confusion. We waited in the station for some time, before we realized that there was no one to assist us, and others were just as confused as we were. We found an unoccupied corner on the third floor of the station to settle in for the night on the cold stone floor, along with many other weary travelers.

Early the next morning while the station was filled to capacity, it became apparent that a scuffle was taking place outside the building. We thought at first it was a fight, as we strained to see what the commotion was all about. In the distance we heard a scream, and as we looked we saw a man being thrown down the stairs from an upper floor by armed bandits. We watched as each step inflicted a blow to his body. Picking the man up again the thugs threw him into the courtyard and shot him.

Everyone was afraid after that. Even though the thugs were outnumbered by the crowds the violent incident paralyzed any possible defense from even the most powerful among the crowd. It was apparent the bandits were inflicting terror by making an example out of that poor man. Some people who were fearful of becoming the next victim fled, while others stood in ashen silence as they were robbed of their possessions.

The bandits continued robbing people throughout the three story building. They would be in our area soon. Being one of the few men left in the crowd I was afraid that I would be shot next. I began to look in earnest for a place to hide. Some of the women recognized my fears and beckoned me to crouch down behind them. They ruffled their long skirts to maximize their width and hid me from sight. I remained hidden there when the robbers entered the room. I did not move a muscle for fear of being discovered.

The robbers shouted to the crowd, "If you know what is good for you, do exactly as I say. We will kill anyone who disobeys our orders." They ordered everyone to place their valuables and money in the robber's sack. They warned again, "Anyone withholding anything will be shot."

The sack was passed among the crowd, each complying with the order. They cut off the finger of a woman who had difficulty removing her wedding ring. The crowd watched in horror, but no one came to her defense. When satisfied with their booty, they left the station. Those in the crowd were traumatized by the experience, and no one could speak.

Ironically the guards in the station had disappeared for the duration of the robbery, and they returned when the robbers had safely departed, as though it had been a conspiracy between them. It was clear that there would be no one with whom we could lodge a complaint.

The train was finally ready to board. The Russian guards milled through the crowds with their guns slung over their shoulders. They barked out an order now and then but did not lift a finger to help the waiting crowd. After boarding the train, we sat in our seats breathing a sigh of relief. Two Russian guards came onto the train and began to inspect the passengers. They stopped in front of us and motioned for me to follow them. I was afraid that I had been chosen to remain there in Poland, and that I would never see my family again. Both Mother and Herta attempted to see where they were taking me. When I looked up I could see them leaning out the window of the train, as I was being led back into the station.

Inside the station I was ordered to help any passengers board the train that could not help themselves. Some were weak and elderly; others were faint from fear, and most were severely traumatized. I mustered up all the strength I had in order to help the frail passengers aboard the train, so I could go back to my family. I could not risk missing the train, as

Mother had my ticket with her. The train had already begun to move, when I grasped the hand rail and swung myself aboard. The relief on Mother's face was clearly evident when they saw me coming toward them.

The train had not reached full speed when we began to cross the threshold of the trestle across the Oder river. We were still in disbelief that we were on our way to freedom. Near the centre of the bridge the train began to slow down, and we became frightened. We thought that the purpose for the stop was to throw us into the river; not one of us could swim. We learned later that all trains crossing the long bridge had to slow down because of the steep grade of the bridge. It was a relief when the train began to pick up speed again.

There was no visible border point between the two countries, but the outcries from the crowded train clearly indicated that we had entered Germany. Some people cheered and others cried. We were overjoyed at the prospect; it was like entering into the Promised Land. We were sure that our life would be better from now on.

Chapter Twenty-One

Angermunde Refugee Camp

We arrived in East Germany in a city called Angermunde. The city was slightly northeast of Berlin. There was a huge refugee camp there, and we were surprised to find that Russians were in charge of the city. We had no knowledge of Germany's defeat in the war or the recent occupation of East Germany by Russia. According to most in the refugee camp, we were in Germany now, and that was all that mattered. Today we were happy to be alive. We were housed temporarily in a large building that appeared to have been used as a military post. When we arrived we were given a colored tag. We carefully guarded these tags, as we recalled our childhood experience in Lodz.

We began to lineup and we were each given a bowl of soup. It seemed like a heavenly meal, and no one complained about the menu. Though we had no promise that our circumstances would improve, and the Lodz camp resembled the one we were in now, we felt that even without father we were a family, and we were determined to stay together.

The Russian plan was to quickly restore order and if nothing else, to repatriate the Germans who chose to remain there. As time went on, there was very little sympathy in the camp for the influx of Germans from the East. There were thousands of people and very little resources. The people arriving in the camp were bruised and exhausted. The people laid down to rest wherever they found an empty corner.

The next morning I awoke to the sound of crowds milling around. There were far more people here than I had ever seen. They separated the women from the men for a customary cleansing procedure that was required of all newcomers to the camp. We were told that there would be a delousing. The men were ordered to lineup, so I lined up with them. The line was now about six persons deep and more than a mile long. The women had a line that was going in the opposite direction. After we entered the bathhouse, we were told to remove our clothes for a shower. Our clothes would be steamed in order to prevent the spread of lice in the camp, then they would be given back to us. They were warm to the touch as we put them back on and left the bathhouse in the same manner as we had come.

After leaving the bathhouse I glanced around, hoping to see anyone I might have previously known in the camp. I wondered if any of my school friends had made it this far. I recognized some from back home in Volhynia and some from Warthegau, and I continued to look for others. The women were required to have their hair shaved as a remedy for head lice before they entered the bathhouse. The barbers waited at the end of each line as one after another the women had their hair shaved.

I looked up and down the lines as we passed, but so far I did not recognize anyone. The people I knew from Volhynia may have gone in ahead of us and were perhaps now long gone. I kept looking for others as we passed. I finally looked up to see a girl that I thought looked familiar. I stopped dead in my tracks not believing what I was seeing. My heart skipped a beat because I knew it was Erna. I still remembered her birthday was the day before mine. How wonderful it was to see her again. I had not seen Erna for more than six years, though I thought of her often. I watched her every move as the line came closer to us.

I began to wonder if she would remember me. There was no doubt in my mind that it was Erna, and it was beyond heartwarming to see her again. The lines continued to move bringing her closer to me with each step we took. As she reached me in the lineup, I could plainly see that she had tears in her eyes. She looked directly at me and began to speak.

"Ferdinand," she said, "they are going to cut off my hair."

I flushed for a moment as I realized that without a doubt she had remembered me. I wanted to comfort her and wipe the tears from her face, but I stood before her, speechless as if I was frozen in a trance. She was sixteen now and more beautiful than I had remembered. I was rudely awakened from the trance by the bark of the guards ordering us to keep moving.

Looking back my eyes followed her as far as I could see, and then she disappeared from my sight. My heart sung with joy! My thoughts of finding her again had wiped out the sadness of my life. I knew I would try and see her again. Throughout the following days I looked for her in earnest throughout the camp, but she was nowhere to be found. I could do nothing more to locate her at this time, but I would continue to search for her as long as I remained in camp.

Everyday at the camp there were new arrivals. Some appeared to have been beaten, others were exhausted beyond description, some collapsed, and some were near death. Those who could stand lined up for their daily rations. No one was meant to stay in the camp for very long. People were being moved out daily, and others were just arriving.

The Russian army guards went through the lines inspecting the new arrivals. We had been in the camp only three days when the guards began choosing some of the stronger men and ordered them to follow. I was chosen among them. We were taken to the front of the line and given our bowl of soup. I wondered what they had in mind in order for us to be favored that way, but I knew better than to ask. I didn't have to wait long to find out the answer.

We were ordered by the guards to go two by two, one at the head and one at the foot to help anyone who could not get up or walk on their own into waiting trucks outside. The guards walked with them and selected each individual. Initially I thought what they were doing was an attempt to help the sick and infirm. I imagined that they would be taken to a clinic or quarantine area where they could be better cared for. It seemed reasonable to me that what they asked us to do was assisting in their care. There were many who were sick, and there was talk that an outbreak of illness could happen.

The trucks pulled away and then returned to the camp empty, and more people were selected. Rumors began circulating that they were being taken to the edge of town. No one would say why, and I began to feel uneasy about the whole operation. I wondered what could be at the edge of town that no one wanted to talk about. I had to find out for myself.

I slipped up onto the seat of the truck beside the driver as the truck pulled away. The driver did not appear to welcome my presence. I tried to make conversation with the man but to no avail. He remained silent, and I could not imagine what had gotten his tongue. The road was dusty and full of ruts. It became a challenge for the driver to stay on course. As we neared the end of the road, I could see a clearing in the distance. It was not long before I regretted that I had climbed aboard the truck that day. The sight of the bulldozers clearing back the earth in the distance took my breath away. I suddenly realized why the driver had remained silent. I couldn't stay here any longer. I jumped from the truck and ran as fast as my legs could carry me back along the dusty road to the camp at Angermunde. I had to make sure my family was safe. I searched frantically for them. When I finally saw them I vowed never to leave their side again. I hid from the guards so they would not realize that I had returned. It would be years before I would reveal the horror of that day. I prayed silently that soon this nightmare would be over.

Leaving Camp

Within a few days the red tags were called which meant that we had been assigned a place to live and that we were on the move again. With each phase of the journey came a sense of relief that we were getting closer to our journey's end.

We arrived in Ponitz, East Germany by train early in the evening. The sun was going down, and we had not yet eaten. As we made our way toward our housing assignment, we could smell the sweet smell of the cooking fires in the air. We passed a farmhouse near the road where a farmer and his wife had been boiling potatoes on the campfire outside. The children were hungry, and they began to beg Mother to ask the farmer to give us a few potatoes to eat. We had not eaten, and hunger overcame our timidity. Mother agreed to ask for a few potatoes, thinking that they wouldn't refuse the children.

Bitte Frau, Ihnen ein paar kleine Kartoffeln für die Kinder ersparen können? *("Please Madam, could you spare some potatoes for the children?")*

"Nein! she said, Die Kartoffeln sind für die Schweine! Was werden wir die Schweine zugeführt, wenn wir Ihnen, Sie geben?" *("No the potatoes are for the pigs, what will we feed the pigs if we give them to you?")*

The children began to cry. On seeing the children cry the woman gathered up a few small potatoes and gave them to Mother.

"Nehmen Sie dies hier, für die Kinder." ("Here, take these for the children"), she said, and we ate the potatoes as though they were a heavenly meal.

The housing that we were assigned had one large room with a small wood stove that was used for heating and cooking. Herta and I would go into the meadow to gather twigs so Mother could make a fire. We would peal bark from the trees and chew it and pick little blades of grass to eat, and in order to stave off hunger pangs we sometimes swallowed bits of sand, pretending it was a fine meal. Being very resourceful, we soon discovered wood beets that were left in the field for cattle. These were tough and stringy, but they could be eaten. The steady diet of wood beets gave us the runs, but it was the only food we had. Before long we began to add other vegetables to the borsch whenever we could find them.

The unfriendly attitude of the people in East Germany was disappointing to us since we had built up high expectations about finally arriving in Germany. We soon realized that even the local residents were struggling against the same hunger and uncertainty that we were. Just like all the others we did our best to adjust to the new life and began to blame most of our difficulties on the war.

Hundreds arrived in the area from the camp at Anger-munde and had to be assigned a place to live. We were under Russian occupation and order was maintained strictly by the Russians, but it was not yet comparable to what it had been in Poland. No one protested openly, and for the time being, peace prevailed.

The Russians would tell us that improvements were coming. We were all afraid to say anything to the contrary. Soon we were given a ration of bread that consisted of one small loaf a week for each individual. If there was a working man in the household, he would be given two loaves. I wasted no time in looking for employment even though no one was paid for their labor in hopes of increasing our bread ration. I left our room early the next day to search for work in the village of Ponitz.

Chapter Twenty-two

Caught in the Claws of the Bear

It had taken half of my lifetime to arrive in Germany. We had come a long way to escape from Russia only to discover Russia was again in charge when we arrived in East Germany. It appeared as though we were caught in the claws of a bear and the bear had a ferocious appetite. It had gobbled up one territory after another in the central European corridor. It would take some time before we could continue working our way to the West. Here in East Germany we had to begin our life again.

Although Russia promised that nothing would change in Germany, I knew from the past that big changes would soon be made. We would have to work very hard to rebuild the unstable economy. I knew from experience that there would probably be forced labor again. I was afraid that there would be very little to look forward to and only more of what we had suffered in the past. My plan soon after we arrived was to find a job even though there was little hope of getting paid in money. I would have to settle for anything I could get. At the moment we only had the allotted bread ration and whatever we could forage in the field along with the clothes we had on our backs.

Within a few days I found a job in a greenhouse. The greenhouse grew small shrubs, trees, flowers, and vegetables. I worked only eight hours every day, and for my labor

I was allowed to take home any of the vegetables that were sorted off to be discarded or baled for animal feed. With the extra bread ration, along with the vegetables I salvaged, we were no longer hungry. Mother even began to preserve the surplus and trade them for other much needed items. Before long we moved into a two room apartment on a farm outside the village. Herta began to work at homemaking for a nearby family, and our life was gradually improving.

I had been used to working from dawn to dusk back in Poland. Here in Germany we worked only eight hours per day, and for the first time I began to grow restless. I was not comfortable with the idle time I had on my hands and thought I could do more. My feelings about remaining here for only a short time had not left me. I would need to earn money if we were to continue our journey to the West, but getting a job that paid money would be difficult.

For the time being life improved, but as history soon would bear witness things would not remain this way for long. For now we could do nothing but remain here in Ponitz, as though once again we were trapped in the Russian zone.

The Hotel in Ponitz

The Russians were known more for their barbarism than for merrymaking, but while in East Germany they were enlightened by the more enjoyable customs of the Germans. A good time with music and dancing was a welcome diversion from war and victory. One evening as I walked the streets of Ponitz looking for work, I passed a hotel dance hall in town and was surprised to see many of the Russian soldiers drinking and dancing there. The Russian soldiers in Poland were never allowed to go dancing, but they all had their share of drinking.

Before the occupation this hotel had been a popular place, and it drew customers from all over Germany. They called the hotel a Guesthause, which was German for hospitality house or dance hall. Those who worked there were paid in money which had gotten my attention. I had been used to working only for food and lodging under forced labor. I thought of how nice it would be if I could get a job in this hotel, even for a very low wage. I could work in the greenhouse in the daytime and work at the hotel at night. I knew however that it was only a dream since you had to dress like a gentleman to work in the hotel at night. I knew that unless I could buy a new suit of clothes there would be no hope of getting a job there. The wretched clothes I wore in the greenhouse were simply not acceptable.

I was downhearted when I returned home that day. When Mother queried me I told her of my desire to work at the Guesthause, but that I needed new clothes. I never dreamed that there was a way to barter at this time. We simply had nothing to offer in exchange. I could not have guessed what Mother had in mind.

The very next day Mother took her ration of bread and some preserves she had made and exchanged it for a couple pairs of pants and a clean white shirt, along with a pair of shoes that had very little wear. I hadn't owned such nice things since I had made the trip to Posnan to purchase a school uniform. I had grown some since then. When I put the clothes on I simply could not believe how good I looked and felt in these new clothes. My confidence was soon restored. It was a good feeling.

I went into town the very next day dressed in my finest. I was hired immediately at the hotel washing dishes, and it was not long after that I was serving the tables in the Guesthause dining room. I was good at serving tables, perhaps because of the skills I had learned at Mother's side back home. Many customers showed appreciation by leaving coins for me. For the first time I saw how beautiful life could be. Also for the first time I was paid a small wage for my work. I looked forward to going back to the hotel each evening after working a full day in the greenhouse.

I loved working at the hotel and looked forward to the evenings of music and merriment. I began to love the life

I now lived, and we improved rapidly. The only music that I had ever known in the past were tunes I made up myself with a worn-out mouth organ I had back in Poland. The hotel played music from America and people danced until it was past the midnight hour. The hotel was very popular and was fast becoming a haven for all cultures where people temporarily forgot the bitterness of their circumstances.

The Russian soldiers arrived at the Guesthause every evening on bicycles they had stolen. Since they were heavy drinkers they would not leave until the hotel closed for the night. They were the most devout customers. They occupied the center of the large dining room which were the best tables in the house. Others occupied the tables at the sides of the room. After an evening of drinking and dancing, they would collect their stolen bicycles and try to head back to the barracks without falling into the ditch.

VERKEHRSHAUS, KONZERT- UND BALLHAUS
MEERANER STR. 2 a PONITZ EAST GERMANY.
FERDINAND SERVED TABLES FOR THE GUESTS
AND SOLDIERS WHO FREQUENTED THE BALLROOM.
IN 1945-46.

I had heard of how the Russians took whatever they wanted from the poor peasants in the village. They bragged about doing so while I served them their beer. After a while I thought of a way to even the score. Every evening as the soldiers arrived, they parked the stolen bicycles in the courtyard. Initially as a joke, I quietly left the hotel, removed several of the bicycles and hid them in a safe place where they could not be found. When the drunken patrons came out to go home, some were without a bicycle. It was late and they were in no mood to walk the distance to the barracks. They would enquire if I had seen them.

I feared for my safety, and I initially pretended ignorance. It was only after they began to offer payment for the safe return of the bicycles that I miraculously found and returned them. While I admitted no guilt for their disappearance, I accepted their generous payment. I soon gained a reputation for my talent in locating missing bicycles. It wasn't long before the military patrons began to offer me money to guarantee their safe return. I was happy that I no longer had to hide the bicycles. The idea caught on. The soldiers were happy, and I was in business.

It would not be long before I made more money from the bicycles than I earned at the hotel.

Chapter Twenty-Three

POW Released

It was late in the year 1946, and the war was over. We were adjusting to the daily challenges in Ponitz under Russian occupation. By this time things were quieting down from the war, and families were being placed throughout the farming districts. We had been promised better housing, and Mother began making new friends. We reestablished a friendship with the Dalke family whom we had known from back home in Volhynia, and it soon became a close friendship.

Lists of those seeking lost family members, as well as POW's released from captivity were being posted in the village square. These lists would assist families with lost loved ones to help find each other. We checked the lists for any sign of Father's whereabouts. Every day we would wait in line down at the village square. Some people had good news when their loved ones were found, while others received news that their loved one had died. We expected the worst while we also entertained a glimmer of hope that Father might still be alive.

Mother began her day by waiting patiently in line. Today was not expected to be any different than any other day, but word had finally come. Mother found Father's name among the list of POWs who had been released. Father had been assigned to a farm in northern Germany and was searching for his family. We were overjoyed. Up until this time Father had no knowledge of our whereabouts, and we wasted no time in writing him.

It wasn't long before the first letter from Father arrived. He wrote that he was treated well while a prisoner. He made new friends and spent idle days trying to keep busy. Upon his release, after a brief time working in forced labor in France, he was allowed to return to Germany a free man.

He was working on the Murke farm; a prosperous farm that had a considerable staff, and the living quarters were clean and comfortable. Father wanted us to come there as soon as we could manage it. He was unable to offer us much help with money since there was little of it to be had. A full year passed as we continued to write back and forth. We kept him informed about our growing savings. We would soon have enough money to continue our journey. We hadn't yet completed our plan to leave East Germany when drastic changes came that would affect us.

By late 1947, fostered by disputes with Russia, currency values dropped, and border restrictions were beginning to be strictly enforced. No one was allowed to cross the heavily guarded border between East and West Germany. People began calling the new border the "Iron Curtain". Rumors circulated that anyone caught crossing the iron curtain would be hunted down with dogs and shot. I had learned from past experience that the rumors were most likely true.

Soon the West instituted a change in currency. East Germany could no longer enjoy equal trade with the West which left the East German currency drastically devalued. Everyone was afraid of the changes that were coming even though Russia promised, "nothing would change in Germany." We applied for papers to cross the border just prior to the beginning of the crisis, and we prepaid our fare in readiness to begin our journey West. This proved to be a very good decision.

Chapter Twenty-four

The Flight Resumes

1947

- The divide between the East and West became known as the "Iron Curtain." Those who attempted to cross the border in spite of the restrictions ended in tragedy. Others who managed to reach safety in the West did so at great risk.
- The East, which included East Germany, Hungary, Bulgaria, Romania, Yugoslavia, and Poland, was controlled by Russia.
- A new currency in the West was introduced.
- The Federal Republic of Germany was born on May 23, 1949. In the upcoming years, the Berlin Wall was built to stem the tide of East German refugees crossing into West Berlin.

The Berlin Wall remained for 28 years until it was demolished in 1990, after which the restriction on travel to the east was lifted. It was more than sixty years before Ferdinand was finally able to return to East Germany to reestablish contact with friends and family there.

The Flight Resumes

We had been in Ponitz for more than a year, and we discovered many people we had known in Poland who had settled in the area. We met them in the town square where lists of those searching for lost family members were posted. We continued to search the lists daily in hopes that other people we knew would appear on them. Mother's friend Anna Dalke from Volhynia had been with us since the refugee camp at Angermunde. They had only just recently found out that her husband was alive as well and stationed near Father in West Germany. Anna and her two children had not been as fortunate as we had been since they had not found employment in the village and had little hope of being reunited with her husband at this time.

The currency crisis began before our papers arrived. We had acted before the deadline, and in doing so we were assured that our papers were secure. We prepared to leave as soon as our papers arrived. Since Franc Dalke had been found, we wanted more than anything for the Dalke family to be able to join us.

I was still working at the hotel in Ponitz when our papers arrived. Mother hurried down to the hotel and asked me to read the contents out loud. The papers stated clearly that seven members of the Golke family had legal passage to the West. Mother could not believe what I had just read aloud and asked me to read it again. Was it possible that the commissioner had made a mistake and sent us two extra passages? Our family numbered only five, but with the two extra passages to the West we could invite the Dalkes to come along.

We had five people in our family and the Dalke family had three. Even though we were now short one passage we would attempt the trip regardless. All eight of us left together the very next day. We boarded the train without incident and settled in for the three day trip west without anyone detecting the error. All eight of us had safely boarded the train, but we were certain there would be many more challenges ahead.

Toward the evening of the third day the train slowed down, and the station at Halle was now in sight. We had to exit the train at Halle, East Germany. This was the end of the line here. When we arrived in Halle the border was closed and heavily guarded. No one was allowed to cross into the West. There were no trains going west, and we would have to find a way to cross the new border on our own.

At the moment we did not know what to do as we had expected to have passage through the border. The last money that we had saved would be of no value in the West. We had no resources for a long stay in the city of Halle. Mother and Mrs. Dalke spent the last of the money to purchase a few buns and a sausage. The crossing point was a few miles to the west of the town of Halle. It would be a distance to walk and more difficult to attempt to cross over. The border to the West was heavily guarded and no one could enter or leave. Warning signs about the dangers of crossing the border were posted everywhere around the station. There were rumors of a tragic attempt to cross the border not more than a day ago. It looked like we had come to the end of the line.

Chapter Twenty-Five

Crossing the Iron Curtain

As we loitered not knowing what to do next, we could hear the cry of the hounds in the distance. It was a bloodcurdling sound and we could only imagine what grizzly duty they could be performing. The sound of occasional gunfire in the distance left us with few doubts about the danger.

We grouped together in the far corner of the station out of earshot from the passersby, in order to plan our next move. We felt it might be necessary to split-up in order to get through safely. We were each assigned a partner. Our next move was to watch the guards as they came and went. Erna Dalke and I were assigned to watch the border for any sign of a flaw in their routine.

Erna and I made our way to the outside of town and found a spot in the underbrush where we could watch from a safe distance. The first day two guards marched back and forth guarding the gate. The dogs arrived early in the evening and remained near the gated road while the soldiers came and went. It was clear that there was no possibility of slipping through without being seen. We returned to the station late in the evening. Mother anxiously awaited our return. There had been no success the first day, and we felt discouraged. Mother reminded us that this would not be easy.

The second day we returned to the hiding place among the underbrush again. We remained there from early in the afternoon until late into the night. Just as the day before, the guards would relieve their post every two hours without a flaw in their routine. I was thankful for Erna's company since the hours in silence watching and waiting was a tedious task.

My companion and I had grown weary and were about to return to the station when shortly after midnight things began to change. The guards at the gate began to share liquor from a flask, and they began to sing and make merry. Their loud boasting and laughter rang out in the darkness. They bragged of their conquests while we watched them and waited. As the night sky was beginning to show streaks of light, the soldiers appeared to be drunk and began to grow restless. The two collected their belongings and disappeared into the darkness taking the hounds with them.

We watched for the replacements to arrive before starting back to the station, but no one approached the gate. We waited and we watched. I had no way of calculating how long it took for the replacements to arrive that night, but one thing was sure. If we had all been there, the entire group could have crossed through the gate that day. Mother was pleased with the news. If that were to happen again the next evening, she said we should make an attempt to cross.

The next day after the sun had set in the evening, we left the station and walked the distance to the growth of trees that hid us from view. We remained there through the evening and into the night. The dogs seemed restless and gave the occasional howl into the night air, but no one paid attention to them. We quietly shared the last of our rations as though this was our very last meal.

Early in the morning long before dawn, the guards began their merriment, just as they had the night before. Our hearts pounded as the morning light began to show in the eastern sky. The guards were due to change, but no one made any attempt to leave, as we had so hoped they would do. Just as we began to think it was all for nothing, the soldiers gathered up their gear, and just as it had been the day before, the drunken guards left their post and took the tethered dogs with them. We waited and listened as they disappeared into the night.

We began to move quietly toward the border crossing. We moved quickly and quietly two by two toward the gate. We passed the warning sign written in German "Gehen Sie nicht über diesen Punkt hinaus!" or "Do not enter beyond this point!" We ignored the sign and began to cross the road. The first to cross was Mother and Erich followed by two of the others, separated only by seconds between them. The last to cross the road was Herta and I. We stared into the darkness in disbelief, because there was still no one in sight. We crossed the road, squeezed under the gate, and ran as fast as we could to catch up with the others.

From now on there would be no time to waste. They would pursue us with the hounds if they discovered we had crossed. The hounds would surely know if someone had passed the gate. The soldiers would soon return, and our lives would be in danger. We had to reach a safe distance before the soldiers returned.

We ran for quite a distance before we stopped to catch our breath. We had gone perhaps a couple of miles, and there were still no signs that the soldiers had returned. We left the underbrush and headed in the direction of the main road. We kept going and didn't look back. We had gone several miles, and daylight was fast approaching when we heard the cry of the hounds in the distance. This would surely mean that the guards had returned to the gate, though no one pursued us. Perhaps it was only the hounds that knew we had passed through the gate that day.

We had finally made it. Against all odds all eight of us had made it through the Iron Curtain. This was a day I would never forget. We had entered West Germany together. I wanted to shout out loud for the victory we had won. I wanted the people to greet us and cheer for us, but there was no one there to receive us.

We continued along the road for several miles before the sun was high in the sky. We had no idea how far we had gone or how long it would take us to reach the nearest village. There were people on the road now, Westerners. Perhaps we could ask them how far it was to the nearest town. We made an attempt to flag down a wagon, but no one would stop. Some appeared to be afraid as they passed; perhaps they thought of us as bandits, or perhaps they thought we were peasants running from the Russians. Others simply hollered out in loud unfriendly voices to keep on going. Maybe in their own way, they were cheering for us after all.

Arrival and Reunion

We reached the town of Goslar near midday exhausted from the journey. We found our way to the train station on the outskirts of town. We all stood together as we presented our papers to the attendant. He was friendly and helpful but asked us no questions. He checked the documents and issued passes for seven people. We crowded together as we boarded the train in the same manner as we had done before. No one counted our numbers. We made our way to the booth at the rear of the train. As the train pulled out of the station and headed north toward the city of Bremen it felt like we were going home. My mind wandered as I sat limply in the booth, and it didn't take long for me to drift off to sleep.

When I finally awoke to the sound of the train whistle, my thoughts quickly drifted from our journey to how good it would be to see Father again. I looked forward to having his recognition and approval for the role I had played in his absence, but I knew he would never know the journey that we had taken.

We had not seen Father since his first leave from the military soon after he enlisted, four years before. I wondered if I would recognize him after all that time. It was just a little more than a day away, and my questions would all be answered. After a short stop at Bremen, the train began to move again. We would arrive in Ofterhalz Sharmbeck before the next evening.

As we approached the station at Ofterhalz Sharmbeck, we could see people waiting on the platform. I was certain that

Father and Mr. Dalke would be there to meet us. We waited our turn to step from the train.

Father was a slightly built man, clean-cut, and shorter than I had remembered him, but I recognized him immediately. Mr. Dalke was tall and slim and looked much older than before. As I had remembered, Father was a conservative man who showed very little emotion and he maintained his composure regardless of the circumstances, but Mother was the opposite. She had tears in her eyes as she greeted Father for the first time in four years.

Perhaps I had become more like Father in his absence which I couldn't help thinking as I stood beside him on the platform. The joy that I wished to express seemed locked up inside of me. It was apparent that it would take time to heal the distance that had grown between us. It would take time to adjust to family life again.

Mother and her friend Anna said their goodbye's at the station and made arrangements to see each other again. We walked the two mile stretch to the farm where Father lived. There we met the Murkes. They were an older couple, slightly heavy-set, but friendly and hospitable. They had a meal prepared when we arrived and asked if our trip had gone well. In an effort not to divulge the horrors we had experienced, we answered their questions in a most jocular manner.

Father's living quarters were clean and bright with electric light and running water. It was cramped for the size of our family, but it would suit us just fine. It was what we needed to help us begin our lives again. Being together as a family gave us a warm secure feeling that things were finally going to turn out right.

Chapter Twenty-Six

A New Beginning By Fate or Determination

After Germany's unconditional surrender, the country was divided three ways, between Russia, France, and Britain/ America. The border regulations dividing the East and West were strictly enforced. The Martial Plan came into effect which brought 12 billion dollars in aid from 1947 to 1951 in order to help in the economic recovery of Europe. The restoration had begun. Returning to the East was now impossible. Later the Berlin Wall was built to further restrict passage to the West. It was not until 1990 when the wall came down that people began to travel to East Germany again with ease.

The war was now over and getting the country working again would take time and planning. The employment situation was bleak, and for me the hope of returning to school was impossible. After the job I had given up in Ponitz, I wondered what this new Germany would offer. I thought about the opportunity that I had left behind in the East.

The devastation from the war in the city of Bremen had left the district in chaos, and the recovery plan was not yet in place. I would have to settle for any work I could get. Convinced that there was no other available work other than farming, I began working on the neighboring farm. The farmer was a large man, very tall and heavy for his frame. He treated me well, and we soon became good friends. He complained bitterly about having no sons to help him since he only had two daughters. They were shy teenagers that were still going to school. We called the girls Martha mouse and Annie mouse because they were so timid.

For a while I was content to work on this farm, as I was treated well there. I was given a generous amount of time to visit my family or to go into town when the work was finished. I had a room where I slept and a washroom of my own. I began to work hard again as it had been my custom to do, even though I took every opportunity to look for work other than farming. I looked for work as far away as Bremen in the south. I had not forgotten my dream of becoming an architect.

While I continued working on the farm, I remembered the life that I had begun in Ponitz. I longed for the music and merriment of the Guesthause Hotel. Even though I was praised for the straight furrows of my plough and the lush rows of green produce I had planted, I felt discontent somehow. I was given good food and lodging but no wages for my labor. I dreamed of things much greater than this.

I continued to work on the farm when one day my "weakness" returned. The farmer insisted that I see a doctor. I stopped working as hard as I once did, and unexpectedly the farmer did not object. He insisted he would keep me with him at any cost, but there was no doubt that my heart could no longer tolerate the heavy labor of farming.

I returned to work as soon as I was able. The farmer would watch for me when I came in from the field and invited me to sit with him. He spoke of his concern for his deteriorating health and how his daughters would inherit the farm. I was not well acquainted with Martha and Anne, although I enjoyed teasing them from time to time in order to make them laugh. I am sure their father had observed this with a watchful eye. I had no love for the farm and I knew then that I would not stay here for long.

To leave the farm I would need a skill. My determination to find one was relentless. I went to butchers' shops, bakeries, tool shops, and the blacksmith shop in the village. The answer was all the same. We have to educate our own people! We have no place for you. Everywhere that I went the answer was the same. I couldn't even contain the disappointment that I felt.

For the first time I felt the sting of rejection. I had not been Polish in Poland, and now here in Germany, I was not considered German. I felt rejected by the country that had offered us hope. I began to think of Erna again, and somehow the thought of her renewed my spirit. I had never forgotten the girl with the beautiful hair that I had known back home in Volhynia. I hoped to see her again someday. I soon recovered from my moment of dejection and decided that tomorrow I would begin my search again.

I walked past a wood shop that caught my attention and began a friendly conversation with Fritz Kettler whom I later found out had taught patternmaking and was the owner of the shop. We took an instant liking to one another. He asked me where I was from and became captivated by the experiences that I told him and of my escape to Germany. Since I had shown so much interest in what he was doing, he took me through his wood shop and showed me his work. I knew nothing of patternmaking, but working with wood somehow interested me. I begged him to allow me to learn his trade. Captivated by my enthusiasm he agreed to give me a try but only under the condition that I left the farm on good terms. At this time farms had the first priority. I was unsure that I could fill the condition that he required, but my heart was set on the new venture. I left his wood shop with a feeling of joy. I would work hard to please the farmer in the upcoming weeks to make sure that he would give me his blessing.

We had no money for the tuition, but I was certain I would come up with a plan. My schoolmaster was agreeable to let me exchange my work for the fees. If I did well I could continue in architecture.

I couldn't wait to tell Father of my good fortune. I expected his blessing when I told him of the new plans that I had made. Surprisingly Father could see no value in pattern-making or my decision to leave the farm. He told me there was nothing wrong with good hard work.

My first assignment was to make a birdhouse out of wood. I managed the task with such inferiority that I was sure that no birds would lay claim to it. If I were to continue, I must apply myself and study hard so that I could improve rapidly. I made friends with an advanced student who became my tutor, and I was eager to learn. Soon thereafter I began to receive good marks.

There was a shortage of suitable dwellings after the war and my schoolmaster began to contract the work of restoring damaged buildings in Bremen. I was given the job of restoring the doors, windows, and stairs in these buildings. We would start from the ground up in order to make them habitable again. We learned and perfected the skills of the masters since our work was checked and rechecked with a critical eye. As my skills improved, I got a better price, and I began displaying my work. I paid my tuition and had some money to spare.

I was never home for long during the first year of my apprenticeship. I spent much of my time in the city where I worked. I even had time to enjoy the nightlife and join others to dance. I took part in stage presentations requiring acting talents and costumes. I began to enjoy my life again. Herta was now sixteen and was allowed to accompany me to the dances on certain occasions, but she was never allowed to go alone. Mother didn't realize that by our prior arrangement, Herta and I each went our own separate ways after our arrival at the dance.

On one occasion I was invited to accompany a young lady for a stroll in the courtyard after the dance. She surprised me with a request for a kiss. I gave her the kiss she asked for, but it was pitifully restricted.

She said, "You kiss as though your heart belongs to another."

I refrained from the exercise for the time being.

Back at class the following day I continued to apply myself. My schoolmaster took note of my enthusiasm for my work and was no doubt responsible for what happened next.

Shortly after my midterm exams, I was approached by a government agent. He acknowledged my high marks in patternmaking and offered me a scholarship in architecture. In my heart I knew that this is what I wanted to do, but first I had to take the last remaining exam. I would tell my parents that very evening. I expected they would be proud of my achievements and opportunity. Unbeknown to me, due to their growing discontent with their circumstances, Father would have his own news to tell.

Chapter Twenty-Seven

End of a Love Story

Germany was just recovering from the war and the first opportunities were to the local citizens. Even though we were German, we were viewed as immigrants, and it appeared that it would take a number of years before our family would be able to prosper here. Even though Father worked hard, very little opportunity existed for farm workers to own a home. I could see that the crowded housing and the concerns for the children weighed heavily on Father's mind.

Mother's Uncle Ernest had immigrated to Canada and he had become a successful fruit farmer. Mother had received a letter from him some time ago, but I had been too busy to inquire of the news it had brought. Today I would have good news of my own to tell. I was certain both Mother and Father would be overjoyed.

When Father learned that I had committed to long-term studies without discussing it with him, he expressed grave disappointment, and Mother began to cry.

"Our plans are to go to Canada," Mother cried. "Uncle Ernest has agreed to sponsor all of us. "This would be our only chance to have a home again and settle in a peaceful land," she said.

I stood bewildered as both Father and Mother spoke persuasively. They said they would not go without me. The family needed me with them once again. While Father was a willing worker, he was uncertain of obtaining employment. He knew nothing of the language and culture of this new land. He had known nothing but farming.

"How could we survive without you?" Mother repeated.

I wanted to refuse, but I could not find the words. I wanted desperately to stay in Germany. I had no idea that my family had made such plans and had already begun to process the papers. My first thoughts were to delay the trip as long as I could in order to finish my apprenticeship. Surely they could understand that.

Just when I began to feel that my life had begun, I would have to leave it all behind. Perhaps there was even another reason, one that I kept secretly within me. Without saying another word I turned and left the house. I needed time to contain the anguish that I felt. I walked out into the night along the railway tracks. I walked for some time without being conscious of the time or the distance, while thoughts of rebellion flooded my brain.

I knew in my heart that I wanted to see Erna again. I had not forgotten her, and even though it had been three years since I had seen her, it was just like yesterday. As I walked along the tracks, I began to remember her again. I wondered if she had survived. If so she would be nineteen just like I was. I knew that things changed over time. She may have married. I knew in my heart that I would never return to the Russian zone, even though it meant that I may never see Erna again. I had to let go of the fantasy I had created. I finally admitted to myself what I had known all along. She was the last vestige of my childhood, the memory that I had held dear had lifted me from the pain of my circumstances and from the depth of my despair. The future was mine; I knew that now was the time to let go of the past.

The hour was late and my parents would be concerned about my whereabouts. I had reached a decision, and I must head back. The evening train would soon be speeding down the tracks toward me. Night had settled in, and the moon shone brightly in the sky. Convinced that I must give up the past and begin my life again, I turned around and began to walk in the direction of home.

Not more than a minute had passed when I was startled by the sound of a pebble that rolled down the embankment along the tracks behind me. It frightened me to think that I might not be alone. I turned quickly to see a naked man following me about thirty feet behind. The man stopped suddenly as I turned to face him. He crouched as if in a defensive pose.

I yelled out to him, "What do you want?"

He ignored my demand and started toward me. Forced to make a quick decision; either defend myself or flee, I turned and began to run. I ran faster than I had ever run. My heart pounded in my ears so loudly that it drowned out the sound of the barking dogs and the snorting of horses beyond the fence along the way.

The man called out to me, "Why are you running? Come back, Please!" he said.

As I continued to run, I wondered about the circumstances of the man, but he had given me a fright and I wanted nothing more than to put distance between us. I looked over my shoulder and saw the growing distance between us until finally he was out of sight.

Up ahead I saw the lights from home in the distance, and I slowed to a trot. As I entered the house, my family was asleep. I quietly removed my clothes that were wet from sweat and slipped between the sheets. The next day Mother woke me for an explanation as to why my clothes were soaking wet. She wondered if I had fallen into the creek. My shoes had to be wrung out and put in the sun to dry. I did not reveal the horror of the previous night, but I did say that I had finally made a decision. I would be going with them to the new land. Mother was joyful at the news.

"I knew you would come with us," she said.

Days later it was reported that a man was apprehended near the railway tracks and charged with an offence. He was later confined to a mental hospital. He was naked at the time of his arrest.

I was more than three-quarters through my apprenticeship when our emigration papers arrived. This was much sooner than I had expected, and our departure would be just weeks away. There was no time left to finish the course that I had worked so hard to accomplish. Not wanting to quit before obtaining my certificate, I approached my schoolmaster to plead with him to allow me to take my final exam. I told him I would need my diploma to find work in Canada. I was willing to do whatever he asked in exchange for allowing me to take the exam.

My schoolmaster had never allowed it before and was sure that I was not ready. He was certain I would fail if I were to take the exam too soon. He paused deep in thought.

When he finally spoke, he said, "You are indeed a very fortunate man. Your ability to accomplish your work has allowed me to recommend you for a very high position in architecture, yet you have turned it down. I had not expected that of you," he said. "However I believe in you, therefore I am going to allow you to take the exam. If you fail, you will not be certified. You will not be allowed to repeat the

course again." He asked, "Do you understand what I am telling you?"

I studied hard, cramming in everything I could learn in the next few weeks. With the help of my friend Jocham, a fellow student in the advanced grade, I readied myself for the exam. I was confident that I was ready when exam day arrived. When the exam was over I learned that I had passed with exceptional marks. My schoolmaster Herr Kettler shook his head in disbelief as he scribbled his signature on my certificate.

"I did not believe that you were capable of such a thing," he said.

I accepted my papers, thanked Herr Kettler for his kindness, and left the school building for the last time pleased with my accomplishment.

Chapter Twenty-Eight

Departure

⌖

Within a few days of my graduation we boarded the train to Bremen where we would certify our passage and spend the last two days before our departure. While in Bremen Mother had arranged for our portraits to be taken which gave her some of the last mementos of Germany.

From Bremen we continued to the port city of Bramer-haufin located in the northernmost tip of Germany, where within a day from now we would board the immigrant ship "Scythia" to begin our trip across the ocean.

This would be a new experience for me, to board a sea-going vessel. I began to feel anxious about the voyage, the ship, its size, and how it stayed afloat. I admired the immense ships that were lined up in the harbor, but as of yet I was not keen on boarding one.

The Scythia was a single-funnel oil turbine ship based in Liverpool, England which touted the same luxury as the most modern ships but on a smaller scale. The gross tonnage of the ship was 19,930 tons, and the ship served a Liver-pool to New York run in the 1920's and 1930's. After WWII Scythia was used to ferry troops across the Atlantic. Beginning in 1948 the ship Scythia became a transport carrier for

CUNARD WHITE STAR SS "SCYTHIA"

displaced persons from war-torn Europe; mainly from Poland and Germany and continued as such until 1958.

We gathered what little belongings we had and stood in
line on the dock at Bramerhaufin. We boarded the ship early
in the afternoon and while my family concerned themselves
with getting settled into their cabin, I had other plans in the
forefront of my mind. I left the cabin to seek out the highest
deck of the ship in order to watch the scenes of the harbor. I
lost track of time as I looked out over the unforgettable view
of Bramerhaufin from the deck of the ship. I stared into the
harbor as far as I could see. A strange sense of sadness came
over me as I thought that I was seeing my homeland for the
last time. I stood for some time on the starboard deck deep
in thought, oblivious to my surroundings as the gangplank
was drawn up and the vessel headed out to sea.

Just as a survivor in mourning, I stood for a moment of
reflection on the deck of the ship. I thought of my grandparents whom I would never see again. I remembered Gerhard
Radky, a special friend who had vowed to remain lifelong

friends, and I wondered if our names still remained in the big oak tree where we had carved them as a symbol of our friendship. I wondered where he was and if he had survived the war. I thought of the kindness of Jozef who had given us enough money to leave Poland. I remembered Adolf Etling who was the owner of the Guesthause Hotel where I hid the bicycles. I thought of Fritz Kettler who had believed in me and taught me a trade. I remembered the blind man in the barn who trusted me and needed me though only for a while.

As the sun was setting with crimson and purple light dancing in the evening sky, I watched the last vestige of Germany slip into the distance, and then I remembered Erna. I remembered our childhood and our chance meeting in Angermunde where I both found and lost her again. I thought of how the war had taken many things from me, but it had also given me something in return. It had taught me determination which enabled me to survive and also gratitude for the little things. It taught me to treasure each member of my family and above all else, it taught me the power of prayer. For these little things I am grateful.

The Scythia had begun to move slowly and gracefully from the harbor, without a single ripple. I saw the shoreline getting smaller in the distance as I stood on deck among the waving crowd. As my eyes strained to capture every last spectacle of the harbor, I knew this would be the last I would see of my homeland and the life I was leaving behind. My throat welled up with emotion and a tear glassed over my eyes. I was lost in my thoughts as I remained on deck for some time until the last vestige of land dropped out of sight. The waves began to get rough as the vessel headed out to sea. The dinner call went out throughout the ship's PA system, and I followed the others down the stairs toward the dining room. I waited to be seated, certain that my family would be joining me there soon.

The first day of our journey was not what I had expected. My family became seasick and had to stay in their cabin. I looked around the ship to find something to do. I climbed to the top and entered corridors and passages that no passenger was allowed to go in. No one restricted me. Finally I began to realize that the dining room was open at all hours. Without the plague of seasickness I returned to the dining room again and again. I ordered anything on the menu that I desired. The waiters stood by eagerly with little to do but serve me. It would take a day or two for the people to recover from their seasickness and then the dining room would be full again. As I was seated at the table and handed the menu, it was a good feeling. I began to taste the luxury that I had not known before.

It was while dining in the ship's dining room that I met a girl named Clair Franc. She was the same age as I was and was traveling alone. Since many of the passengers had not yet recovered, Clair and I spent many hours there while the waiters served our every whim. Within the first couple of days on the ship, we developed a close friendship. One day near the end of our journey, we discovered a quiet place on the deck of the ship where we laid back and watched the billowing clouds go by as the ship rose and fell in the giant waves. It was a sweet adventure as I held her in my arms.

About midway on the seven-day crossing of the Atlantic, we encountered a fierce storm and had to cast anchor for several hours. The storm sent most of the frightened passengers to the confinement of their cabins, but I was unaffected. The wilder the storm got, the more enthralled I became. It soon passed and we began to move again.

After the sixth day on the ocean, we entered the Gulf of St. Lawrence and caught the first glimpse of the Canadian coastline and the beginning of the St. Lawrence Seaway. The rocky shoreline of Newfoundland was a sight to see. The cliffs broke the water and towered above us. We could see icebergs in the gulf and a school of whales spouting a safe distance away. Continuing down the St. Lawrence River we passed many seagoing vessels. There were ships larger than the Scythia, some with three and four stacks. The freighters slid through the giant waves with ease filled to the brim with coal and iron. The islands along the way, which were mostly uninhabited, gave way to romantic fantasy as Clair and I stood together on the upper deck of the ship naming them as they passed

On the seventh day Quebec City was now in sight. We would soon leave our cabins and begin to disembark. We were given our landing pass for a tourist third-class. Our landing instructions were clearly printed in bold red lettering in several languages.

This was where Clair and I had to part. While Mother and Father had recovered from their seasickness and were glad to see their journey end, surprisingly I longed for it to continue. Clair would leave the ship before us and complete her journey to Toronto, Ontario by bus. We walked together for as long as we were able before we had to say goodbye. I felt in my heart that in a short while I had grown fond of Clair. We exchanged addresses and promised each other that we would write.

We landed in Quebec City, Canada, October 3, 1949. I began to feel a great sense of adventure returning to me as it had done many times before. I was twenty years old and excited that our new life had just begun. I was eager to embark on this new venture and was determined to work hard to succeed. I put the past life behind me and contemplated the future optimistically.

Phase II

An Immigrant Family in a New Land

Chapter One

Oh Canada

⌒

We disembarked from the ship Scythia and went through customs at the Canadian Port of Quebec in Quebec City, Canada, where our papers and medical authorization were examined and stamped, *"Approved for entry, October 3, 1949."* Due to the number of German-speaking passengers, we were instructed by an attendant speaking in German and French to board a bus that would take us to the next phase of our journey. On the bus we were given our tickets to western Canada, along with $5.00 per person in Canadian money. This was to help cover the cost of food until we reached our destination. I did not know what the value of the money was, or how long it would take to reach British Columbia, but Father would make sure that it covered the needs of our trip, of that I was certain.

I was surprised at the number of German- and Polish-speaking people that had immigrated along with us. Many boarded the same bus as we did and were also traveling to western Canada. I wondered how long the next phase of the trip would take us, since I knew very little about this beautiful new land we would now call our home.

It was a short trip by bus through Quebec City where we would board the train destined for western Canada and Uncle Ernest, who awaited our arrival. While passing through the city, I couldn't help but notice the architecture of the buildings which to me resembled France.

We boarded the train and our next stop would be in the city of Winnipeg, Manitoba, which I was surprised to find would take approximately three days travel. There was a great deal to learn about this new land, I thought. We could buy food on the train whenever we were hungry, but Father feared spending any money. He was determined to arrive with money in his pocket. We would have to make do with the food we had brought from the ship.

Since I was the adventurer in the family it did not take long before I left my family's side to discover every inch of the train. I went from the engine room at the front all the way to the caboose. I walked the narrow hallways and stood on the decks between the cars looking at the scenery of the rugged Ontario northland as it went whizzing by. As I stood on the deck of the train I could not help but think of the time I escaped from the military. The trains here seemed to be much faster I thought. With long periods of travel with nothing but bush land and no real signs of civilization, the monotony was getting the better of me. I was anxious to discover civilized Canada by the time the train pulled into Winnipeg. The family agreed to allow me to slip off the train to buy food in the city. The price of food there would be much more reasonable than on the train, and by now we were ready for a hardy meal.

I headed for the downtown area of Winnipeg where I found a butcher shop and purchased buns and sausage to take back to the train with me. I did not suspect that Winnipeg was such a large city, and I became distracted by the new sights and sounds of it. I lost track of time, and I could not remember my way back. I had no fear since it seemed to me that I had been in this predicament before. It would be a simple matter to ask for directions from a passerby. I had forgotten that I could not speak a word of English. I approached people in passing, asking for directions to the train. Absolutely no one could understand a word that I was saying. I was now lost in the city of Winnipeg without my landing papers, and I could not speak a word of the language. The train would leave the station soon, and I did not know where this British Columbia was. If I missed the train I knew I was in trouble. I had to think hard and try to retrace my steps without the assistance of anyone. It took longer than I had expected, but I finally found my way back to the station without much time to spare.

To my astonishment upon my arrival, the train was no longer where it had been when I left that morning. Surely it had not left the station earlier than scheduled. I knew what a problem it would be if the train had left without me. Mother had all my papers, and I couldn't speak the language. The only consolation was that thanks to my trip into the city, I had enough food for a day or two. I looked around at all the trains that were coming and going through the station, but my family was nowhere to be seen and there was no sign of our train.

I thought I was hearing things when out of nowhere I heard Mother and Herta calling my name. I looked up and saw them waving at me from the coach, a number of tracks over, where the train had been disconnecting cattle cars and adding another engine in preparation for the next phase of the trip through the Rocky Mountains of western Canada. What a relief I experienced as I boarded the train. Mother immediately insisted that I carry my own immigration documents from then on in the event that I would, "try this trick again." After my experience in Winnipeg, I was determined to learn English and would make it my first priority.

Western Canada was nothing like Europe since Europe was far more densely populated. After leaving Winnipeg there were miles and even days between the small towns and villages. The Rocky Mountains were magnificent. The train whistled as it rounded steep bends that exposed deep canyons below. We saw wildlife grazing on the sides of the mountains. What a lonesome, vast country this Canada was. We had one more stop in Kelowna. Having learned my lesson, I did not leave the train. We were still a half day's journey away from Vernon, the town where Mother's uncle lived.

When we arrived in Vernon we climbed down from the train onto the small wooden platform and looked around to see if anyone was there to meet us. A young man stood near an automobile waiting and he called out our name. He introduced himself as Walter Breitkreutz, and said he was Uncle Ernest's son. We would ride in his auto to Uncle Ernest's home. We all crowded in, with Erich and Frieda seated on our laps.

The roads were made of gravel, but the highways were paved. The scenery was spectacular. Mountains jutted up high into the air from both sides of the highway. We passed a beautiful lake on the right. We were headed toward the valley that was situated between two mountain ranges. All along the valley there were miles of lush green fruit trees. This place was a marvelous sight.

We arrived at Uncle Ernest and Aunt Olga's farm located slightly northeast of the town of Vernon. The lane was lined with fruit trees on both sides. There were outbuildings and fruit-packing sheds located near the road. We remarked that Uncle Ernest had done well since he had come to Canada. His son told us that he was one of the largest fruit growers in the area. We came to a stop near the front door.

The home was an immense three story building with many gables and with windows that overlooked the valley. Uncle Ernest and Aunt Olga stood at the door to greet us. They led us to the great room where all the guests gathered to the right of the large entrance. This was the most magnificent room that I had ever seen. The fireplace went from floor to ceiling, two stories high. From the ceiling of the large dining room hung a massive chandelier, and the room was furnished with a table that could accommodate their large family as well as many guests. I had not seen any house that compared to this. I carefully observed every inch of the structure, taking note of its construction and fabric. I would build a house like this one day, I thought.

We were introduced to many family members whom we had never met before. They had all gathered at the home to meet us. We had no trouble at all fitting in since all the guests spoke German. We learned that many other German families had settled in Vernon as well. Some had arrived in the late 1800's. We learned that some new immigrants had become full-fledged Canadian citizens. It had not been possible to become a citizen of a new land in Europe, or so I had been lead to believe. There would be a great deal to learn in the next few months, of that I was certain.

The next day our family was given a small four room cottage on Uncle's farm not far from the main house. It was adequate for our immediate needs and we were happy to begin our new life there. The harvest was beginning so we made ourselves useful and began picking fruit on Uncle's farm. Father would not take payment for the labor since he thought it was only fair to help in lieu of any rent that we would owe. He would see to it that we were not a burden on Mother's family and hoped that we could soon become independent.

We had no money except for what had been given to us at the Port of Quebec which Father held on to with a tight fist. The last of the money would have to be spent on a large bag of flour and a couple of large bags of potatoes. We were welcome to use any fruit and vegetables that grew on the farm and together with the staples that we had purchased we thought we were living well. We had not had it this good since we left Warthegau in 1944, five years before.

Chapter Two

New Beginning

⌘

According to reports Canada was still experiencing the effects of the Great Depression, even though it had begun in 1929. As a young man I had not personally felt the sting of it, since it had always been difficult for us in Europe. Now there was a new challenge, because we could not speak the language. There were very few jobs in Canada for the working man with a family. Skilled tradesmen were in short supply. Within days of our arrival a bus was sent to pick up any skilled tradesmen who had recently arrived from Germany. If they were qualified, they would be given jobs in the lumber industry in Trail, British Columbia, which was a smelting and lumber town about forty miles from Vernon. With my trade certificate in hand, I got on the bus. I was hired immediately and given temporary residence which was a room that the company had rented for their workers. Because I could read blueprints, I was given a more responsible position in the plant and better pay.

The nine hour days flew by fast, and I had little to do in the evenings. I had to learn English so I bought an English newspaper every week and began to translate, one word at a time, in an attempt to learn the language. I struggled on my own every day to add new words to my vocabulary, but I was not satisfied with my progression. I thought there had to be an easier way. Things began to improve when I volunteered to babysit the supervisors' children while they went out in the evenings. While the children did their homework, I did my homework along with them. The children would correct my work and laugh at me when I spelled my words wrong.

They would remark with glee, "Look at him, he is a grown man, and he can't even spell the words."

The children became my tutors and with diligence I could speak, read, and write English within three months. I was given a promotion at work along with an increase in pay as a result.

In the mill we made window frames and moldings of all sizes. We also made some furnishings, and we even made pews for the church. I knew my job well, and since I was familiar with all the intricate tooling, I became a project planner almost from the onset. I had never regretted the skill that I had so laboriously accomplished in Bremen, and it was now paying off. I began to advance, and as I gained confidence I made suggestions that improved production which got the attention of the owner. I was treated to hockey games after hours as a reward. For the first time I saw the Canadian game of hockey played in a sports arena. I began to love this new land.

The language barrier affected many of the immigrant men and they were without work for months. After my first trip home, I returned to Trail with five men from Vernon including Father. There was plenty of work in the lumber industry of which the mill was a part of. All of the five men who accompanied me were hired by the mill where I worked. Father never uttered a word to me about farming from that time on.

There was no available housing in Trail at this time. My next challenge would be to find a place for the six of us to live in the town of Trail. While walking along the street I observed a newly built home with a heated garage at the back. I stopped to talk to the owner who was attempting to finish the woodwork in the home that he had recently moved in to. He expressed concern that he may not have the skills to finish the fine carpentry and the cabinetry that remained undone. I immediately offered to do the work for him if he would allow my father and I and the others to stay in his heated garage for the winter. The man was elated and agreed to the deal. We now had a place to live rent free.

I worked at the mill during the day and did the fine wood-work in the house in the evening. I worked with diligence and relentless enthusiasm as though the house were my own. In short, I loved to work with wood. The homeowner was pleased with the results and allowed us to stay on after the work was done for a very small fee.

One weekend per month the men would return home to spend a couple of days with their family. During one of my trips home to Vernon, I borrowed a Holy Bible from Uncle Ernest's library hoping no one would discover that it was missing. I read the book through from cover to cover on two different occasions before I returned it to the shelf. I learned many things from the experience. It was the very beginning of my desire for a godly lifestyle that influenced every aspect of my personal life from that point on.

In 1949, Canada had come through the Great Depression and even though the labor unions were gaining strength, the wages were poor, the top wages being no more than $1.50 per hour.

Since I was still living by the economic standards I had known in Poland, spending money on frivolous purchases was out of the question. I spent $10.00 for groceries, and the rest that I earned was allocated for savings. My grocery purchase consisted of canned meat, cereal, bread, and potatoes, which would last me the month. This amount of food was considered heavenly by the standards that I had been used to. I apportioned each meal, and I thanked God for the provisions he had made for us in this new land.

My savings began to mount up. When I returned to the store to purchase the next month's rations, the storekeeper asked me why I did not buy all of my groceries there.

I told him, "This *is* all of my groceries!"

I looked for other things to do to earn money. I began to put my patternmaking skills to work again. With salvaged lumber from the plant scrap bins I began to build a boat. The owner had allowed me some unused space in the plant where he carefully observed each phase of the boat's construction in interest. I added a motor, a steering column, and a steering wheel. The owner was visibly impressed.

News of my boat-building skill began to spread, and when the boat was finished there were buyers anxiously waiting in line. It would be sold to the highest bidder. I merely had to demonstrate the boat's seaworthiness by taking the new owner out on the lake. I was confident in my skills and eager to do so even though I had not learned to swim.

I soon discovered the demand was high for pleasure boats, and being pleased with the success of my first project I began to make a second one. Just as the first boat had, this too was sold immediately. In less than six months I had accumulated a considerable sum of money. While I had worked hard for this money, I had no real joy of owning it. I began to think of what I could do with it. With much deliberation I finally came up with a plan, but I needed to ask Father's opinion.

The men had been working for a few weeks now and wanted to return home for a visit with their families. I went along with them and arrived there late in the day. I was happy to see our family was doing well. Herta began to work, and Mother had accumulated a few new things. The highlight of my trips home was enjoying Mother's home-cooked meals which I considered a real treat. The following day Father and I went to Uncle Ernest's home to talk over some business. Uncle Ernest seemed surprised to see us and didn't suspect the nature of our visit. He led us to the dining room where the huge table graced the center of the room.

"Please, sit down," he said.

We came to the point of the meeting quickly. I asked Uncle Ernest how much it had cost him to sponsor our family. He was reluctant to reveal the amount it had cost, since we had spent time working for him on the farm.

After Father insisted Uncle Ernest reveal what the fare had cost him, he told us that it had cost two thousand dollars. I sat down and made out a check in the amount of two thousand dollars and handed it to him. He looked surprised as well as confused as he glanced down at the check in his hand.

He then looked up at us and asked in disbelief, "Where did you get this money?"

I answered, "I earned it."

"That is impossible," he said, and repeated again, "Where did you get this money?"

He was speechless for a few minutes while he pondered how anyone could earn that kind of money in a country where the top wages were $1.50 per hour. The country had suffered a depression and was only now beginning to recover.

Even though Uncle Ernest and Aunt Olga had a large family of their own, they found a way to help other family members in need. Though stern in character Uncle Ernest had demonstrated that he was a fine man of heart. We never forgot the sacrifices they had made on our behalf and remained grateful forever.

Chapter Three

Going East

❧

After obtaining employment in Trail, I remained there for several weeks. On the first opportunity that we were given a short leave, I returned home to find several letters from Clair had arrived. She had apparently adjusted well to the city of Toronto. She learned to speak English and had found employment in homemaking. We had exchanged addresses on board the ship and I had promised to keep in touch once I was settled. I had misplaced her address and because I wanted to settle our family debt, I had not immediately written Clair as I had promised, even though I had every intention of doing so. I sat down and answered each letter, giving her my new address in Trail.

Since my arrival in the West, I still wanted to further my education and had written several universities in the East for information on courses in architecture. Upon reestablishing a close friendship with Clair it looked as though I might be going east far sooner than I had expected.

Clair and I continued to exchange letters frequently and in doing so I believed something more than a casual friendship had developed between us. It had been more than a year since we parted that memorable day on board the ship Scythia. I began to think of how good it would be to see her again. She expressed no interest in coming west but seemed pleased if I would come east instead which suited me very well. My sense of adventure was returning to me. Father disapproved of my decision to leave the family and thought I was throwing caution to the wind.

On the train coming east, I revisited places that I had previously experienced and none had been more memorable than Winnipeg. This time while I could venture safely into the city, I chose to remain close to the station for the entire four hour stopover. When I arrived at Union Station in the city of Toronto, Ontario, my first thoughts were to find a room before contacting Clair. I rented a room in Rosedale and spent my first night there.

I awoke early the next morning. I wanted to meet Clair again and be able to spend the next several months there, so I decided the next step was to try and find a job.

I took the subway from one end of the city to the other. Each stop I made showed promise. It was certain that Toronto had far more opportunities than there were in the West, I thought. I ended up at the Queen Street subway station where I had been the night before. I walked into the Eaton's building in downtown Toronto to inquire about employment. The manager took real interest in my accomplishments and offered me a job with the same pay that I had gotten in Trail. I would start the next day. Now I was happy that I had something to offer a girl if I needed to.

I contacted the residence where Clair had been working and she arranged to meet me that evening. I counted the hours.

My first glimpse of Clair left me a little faint. I had looked forward to this moment and could not account for my sudden lack of courage. Instead of a jubilant rekindling of the friendship we began on board the ship, I greeted her with a handshake and Clair shyly kept her distance. After a brief mention of how pleased she was that I had come, Clair put her arm in mine and directed me to a streetcar that would take us to a small coffee shop along Queen Street in the city where she had often spent leisure time.

I was thrilled to see her, but something about her seemed different. I was at a loss for words and couldn't think of where to begin the relationship again. Clair appeared much older than I had remembered her. I reached up to help her as she stepped from the streetcar to the platform in the center of Young and Queen Streets. We crossed the street and walked another block to a well lit coffee shop that was located on the corner. We entered and sat down. Then we ordered from the menu but I was too nervous to eat.

Clair asked about my family and about my trip east. She lamented that it had taken so long for me to write. She said that many things had changed in her life since we had parted nearly two years before. I began to think, had it really been that long. The time had gone by much faster than I had realized, and I could sense that things were no longer the same between us.

As we continued to share our experiences I began to realize that in spite of her letters to the contrary, Clair had withdrawn from our romantic friendship. Hoping to solicit my full understanding, she continued to tell me of the trials she had gone through and the loneliness that had driven her. A relationship had subsequently developed, and she wanted my blessing.

I listened intently to her story but couldn't help feeling that she did not reflect the happiness that she expressed. Convinced that Clair would stand by her decision, I had to believe that she had probably made the right choice. As I accompanied her back to her flat that evening, I couldn't help thinking that I would be leaving the city much sooner than I had planned. I could only reflect on Father's parting words, about throwing caution to the wind, and that he had been right all along.

I left Toronto for Windsor in the spring of 1951. I looked up friends that I knew, and soon after my arrival a reception was held which was the custom among the German immigrant families. This is where I met Elfriede Streich. Elfriede was a quiet spoken, attractive girl who easily captured my attention. We had many experiences to compare. She was one of the younger members of the large Streich family and had fled Poland after the war. We spent many hours together healing each other's wounds of the past, and we became close friends. In no time at all I recovered from the loneliness of leaving my family and the disappointment I experienced in coming east. After a courtship lasting several months, Elfriede and I married on December 22, 1951 at the age of twenty-two. We made our home in Windsor, Ontario in order to be close to Elfriede's family. Over the course of time we had three children, Norbert, Gerhard, and Cathy. My wife Elfriede and I became dedicated to God together and were baptized by water immersion in Chatham, Ontario in 1966. We lived and worked side by side for forty-five years before Elfriede's untimely death due to breast cancer.

More than sixty years have passed since I escaped from certain doom in the land of my birth. In reflection I reassemble those days with an element of sadness. The people that I once knew, the friends that I made, the common bond we carried from this time of trouble, strengthened those who survived and left others by the wayside. Those few short years during trying times while infinitesimal in the span of human history, were so significant in affecting the world long after the war was over. Individuals who suffered through these perilous times came from many nationalities. Some, like our family were fortunate to be able to build their life again.

Long after the sting of the past had healed over, I was reminded once again of these frightful times when a worker in my crew spoke up boldly saying, "In the war we were shooting you Germans, and now you come and give us orders again."

When asked of my regrets, I can recall only one, for the ones I left behind.

~The End~

The Guesthause Hotel in Ponitz, East Germany

Ferdinand and Herta returned to East Germany in the year 2001. They revisited the village of Ponitz.

By chance, while walking on the street, we met Siegfried Etling, the son of Adolph Etling, the owner of the Guesthause Hotel where I had worked serving tables more than sixty years ago. We spoke in front of the very location where the Guesthause Hotel had once stood. With tears in his eyes Siegfried Etling spoke of the fate of the hotel and the changes that affected him and his family after the Russians took over East Germany. He went into his dwelling for a brief moment and retrieved a postcard that showed the hotel as it had been before the war. He gave it to me in memory of my experience.

Siegfried said, "Early in 1950 my father's money and property were seized; the hotel was shut down and later demolished. The reason for the drastic action was that the hotel played western music."

Western music had been banned in Russia.

He continued, "One of the drastic measures taken under the new communist government was to do away with personal wealth and make everyone equal. My father was well-known in the community as you know. Taking action against him would serve as an example to others not to pursue personal wealth under communism."

After his property and bank account were seized, Siegfried's father Adolph Etling was forced to do hard labor until
his premature death in an impoverished state.

While I remained in the area, I visited the small country
graveyard in Ponitz where I stood in silence by the grave-
stone of the man that had helped me those many years ago ...
and remembered.

Emma Golke (Mother): She recovered well from the
burns she had received in Poland and fulfilled her lifelong
dream to "settle in a peaceful land". She grew to enjoy her
new life in Vernon, British Columbia, Canada, where she became grandmother to several grandchildren. Her legacy was
creating beautiful flower gardens, and she was also notori-
ous for making the best sauerkraut. She became the foster
parent to a beloved grandchild after the premature death of
her daughter Frieda. Emma Golke passed away October 26,
1978, at the age of 70 after a prolonged illness.

Emil Golke (Father): He gave up farming after coming to Canada. He began working immediately and settled
in well in the community. Emil and Emma purchased their

first home soon after arriving. Emil worked in various oc-
cupations locally in Vernon, British Columbia, and at a lumber company in Trail, B.C. until his retirement in 1959. He
showed a tremendous interest in the Canadian justice system
and would spend many leisure hours viewing court cases
in the county courthouse in Vernon. Emil passed away suddenly in 1978.

Herta Golke: She married Adolf Holland who had emigrated from East Germany. The young married couple settled in Vernon, British Columbia and raised four children,
Irma, Rose, Herald, and Arthur.

Herta was a diligent worker and had a variety of jobs, including that of a binary operator, and she spent a number of
years working in the fruit-packing industry. Herta remained
close to our parents, attending to their needs in their elder
years. Herta's husband Adolf Holland worked in the logging

industry as an industrial logger before his retirement. Herta and Adolf live in British Columbia, Canada.

Frieda Golke: She married Eckhart Merke and bore two daughters, Irene and Barbra. Frieda died from unknown causes in 1959, at the age of twenty two, shortly after the birth of their youngest child. The family grieved deeply at her passing. Her two children were raised by their grandparents after the sudden tragic death of their father Eckhart who died in a work-related accident.

Erich Golke: He married Sherrill Webster and bore four children, Rick, Steven, Debbie, and David. Soon after his marriage Erich left British Columbia for Ontario to join Ferdinand, where he served in an apprenticeship in carpentry. Erich and his family later returned to British Columbia, where he worked for a time in his trade, later accepting a position as a hotel maintenance manager until his retirement in 2008.

The Dalke family: After accompanying the Golkes through the Iron Curtain, the Dalkes, were reunited with their family and remained near Bremen, West Germany

Gerhard Radky: After Gerhard and I made a friendship pact, we parted due to the fact that we were assigned to a different branch of the military. After the Russians began to occupy Poland in the war, my two friends Gerhard Radky and Helmit Schindler, were captured and remained in confinement until the war was over. After the war was over, they were not immediately released. As a training exercise for the dogs, the Russians released only one or two of the young men at a time. After a short time in order to give the men a head start, the tracking dogs were let loose to track where they had gone. The more fortunate ones managed to escape while others were brutally recaptured. There were only a very few able to outwit the dogs. When they were captured they were beaten and mauled by the dogs. Some did not survive the attack.

Without any knowledge of the exercise my friends were told that it was their turn to be set free. Before they left the camp, Helmit was taken into confidence by a Jewish man who secretly informed him of the trap. Helmit refused to go. Gerhard having freedom in the forefront of his mind, left the compound thinking he could outwit the dogs if given a head start. It was not long before he was caught, and he was beaten into unconsciousness. No one knew what had happened to him. Soon thereafter, as was the custom when a soldier was missing in action, Gerhard's mother was sent his death notice along with his tag and belongings. It was believed that Gerhard had died while on active duty. Five years later the family received a letter from him informing them that he was alive and had spent several years in a military hospital healing from his wounds and the trauma he had suffered. He recovered poorly and remained frail for the remainder of his life. He never married and later passed away before his time from the effects of the injuries he had received.

Erich Echner: Erich and I had parted company after fleeing the military together. We never heard from Erich again throughout the remainder of the war. The rumor that he had immigrated to Canada remains unconfirmed.

Erna Shmitkey: We had no further contact with Erna and her family after leaving the refugee camp at Angermunde. We learned several years later that Erna and her mother had remained in the vicinity of Guesnets, East Germany near Ponitz. Though unknown to us the Shmitkey family arrived in Ponitz shortly after we did, and by some coincidence had lived within a few miles of us.

Erna and her family remained in East Germany where she married and raised a family. After locating her through mutual friends, I longed to meet up with her again. My wife Elfriede and I planned a trip to East Germany in 1990 when travel there was no longer restricted. The trip was delayed due to poor health. Several years later in 2001, I arranged to make the trip again. I arrived in Guesnets only to discover that Erna had passed away within months of my arrival. It was comforting to learn that my friend from long ago had embraced the same faith as I had and entertained the same hope of future resurrection.

Ferdinand Golke: As told by a family friend. He married, Elfriede Streich in December 1951. Soon the family grew to have three children, Norbert (Justin), Gerhard, and Cathy-Anne. In time Ferdinand and Elfriede became grandparents to seven grandchildren. Ferdinand began his career in building construction soon after arriving in Ontario. He enjoyed many years in all phases of construction, which included the building of medical clinics, schools, office buildings, auto assembly plants, distilleries, and the expansion of the University in Windsor before his retirement in 1994. After the death of his wife Elfriede due to breast cancer, Ferdinand remarried. He and his wife reside in Ontario.

Family History

The Golke Family's Ancestral Sojourn from Prussia

In the eighteenth century, Prussia was a vast territory. At its core was the principality of Brandenburg. It was the center of German culture for several hundred years. Poland lay to the east and south of Prussia.

Historically, while living in Prussia our German ancestors were hardworking people of the land, either serfs or farmers, and as such, could not own property. They made their living by means of hard manual labor and gleaned what they needed for their survival from what they could gather from the fields and from what was apportioned to them in payment for their skills. In the most part they were God-fearing people with a high regard for the Holy Scriptures. This manner of life instilled in them a conservative nature that often defined their German culture. In order to survive when times were tough, money earned was never spent frivolously.

In the 1800's as the population grew in Prussia, there were fewer prosperous farms that could accommodate the needs of the growing population, forcing people to migrate to the South and East where fertile land were more abundant. In some historical records there was mention of wagon trains carrying people from Prussia to Volhynia, Poland in the early- and mid-1800's.

The "Partitions" of Poland during the 1700's imposed political divisions which weakened the united resolve of Poland for more than 100 years. During the partitions, Poland was divided in three parts and dominated by three different nations, Russia, Austro-Hungary, and Prussia. Each nation had strong political aspirations and influence. This divided Poland's growing population and kept its borders in constant dispute. It was not surprising that countries surrounding Poland became ever watchful for a chance to take its wealth.

Caption: 1914-1934. Poland had arisen once again from the previous struggles, but even in doing so had not earned recognition as a country. It was not until after the First World War that Poland won the right to govern itself politically and was promised support and backing. Even so this did not secure the peace that was promised. Both Germany and Russia hovered hungrily over Poland's territory.

In the early 1900's Poland was rebuilding itself from the devastation of the "Partitions" and rulers throughout Poland encouraged colonization as many hands were needed to build a new land. Communities were formed and a sense of solidarity existed amongst the villages. Many German families came to Volhynia from Prussia by means of wagon trains, yet little is written about them, their families, or their circumstances.

Poland was endowed with rich agricultural land, timber, and other valuable resources that attracted new settlers who were hoping to build a new life. Though colonization was encouraged, the newcomers were not recognized as citizens of Poland and therefore kept their own national identity and customs. For more than two generations the Golke family enjoyed peace and prosperity in the district of Volhynia. The rural village of Jachimufka located to the South and East along the border of the Ukraine was far from the line of fire during the First World War. Very little is known about Volhynia since political adversity and rapidly changing borders removed it from modern maps.

The Golke Family History

In honor of the Golke family, the following Golke Family History has been recorded. With pleasure the author presents it in conclusion.

Ferdinand's grandfather, Gottlieb Breitkreutz, on his mother's side, gained prominence by contributing many talents to village life. He was well-known for making leather harnesses for horses, as well as wagon wheels and sleds. He later carved wooden clogs and was known for the invention of a type of weaving apparatus that was used to make blankets out of wool. With these much needed skills he became well-known throughout the district. The following picture has been inserted showing him in his advanced years. Due to a scarcity of easily accessed pictures of the family, the following photo shows the three Breitkreutz brothers who were reunited in Canada after the war. Gottlieb Breitkreutz is the father of Emma Golke and is the Golke children's maternal grandfather.

Ferdinand's father Emil Golke was born in Jachimufka, Volhynia in 1905. He was the youngest of five siblings. At the age of 21 he married Martha Bruksch. Martha was a close friend of the Golke family. Martha had a daughter named Hilda, who was four years old at the time of her marriage to Emil. The union came to a tragic end when Martha died during the stillbirth of the couple's first child. After the death of her mother Martha, young Hilda was raised by her maternal grandparents who lived in the next village. Since the children of several villages attended the same school, Ferdinand was able to acquaint himself with Hilda, but knew her only as a cousin. Ferdinand said they lost track of Hilda through the war. Family members eventually located her years later and a kinship with her was rekindled. Hilda had grown up near Hanover, Germany, married and bore twin sons and a daughter. Hilda and her husband are now deceased. The

Brothers Reunited

Three brothers met for the first time since 1909 last week, when Ernest Breitkreutz of Dawson Creek, right, and Julius Breitkreutz of Edmonton came here to visit their brother, Gottlieb, in bed, who arrived from Germany earlier this year. The Breitkreutz family were born in a German-speaking area of Russia prior to the First World War. Ernest and Julius emigrated to Canada in 1909, while their elder brother remained behind and experienced two world wars in which he lost everything he owned. In the second conflict he was displaced to West Germany. His wife died last year and his own family, who had previously emigrated to Canada, persuaded him to follow. He is a guest of his daughter, Mrs. Emil Golke of Vernon. The visiting brothers are guests of their niece, Mrs. Louis Hennig of this city. When they arrived here they found Gottlieb in bed, suffering from ill health that has dogged him since his arrival last spring.

children, Gerald, Gerhard, and Marlis presently reside in Hanover, Germany.

At the age of twenty-three, Emil who had been widowed two years before married again. His new wife Emma Breitkreutz, who later became Ferdinand's mother, brought with her remarkable domestic abilities and a firm determination to succeed. Emma was born in 1908 in the village of Mankov, Volhynia, one of the oldest in a family of nine children. She had no formal education, though she was strong and hard-working and managed a household well. In the early 1900's girls did not attend school but were taught homemaking skills, housework, needlework, cooking, and childrearing, which assuredly would attract them good husbands.

In 1928, Emil and Emma salvaged their share of the huge oak timbers that had been abandoned from the dugouts of WWI, in order to build the framework of their new home. Many people stopped by to see the home which Emil took great pride in showing off. The new home included a cellar enabling them to store food for the winter since refrigeration was not yet in common use. The village of Jachimufka was initially a Polish settlement with some influence from the Ukraine, which lay to the East. Later with the vast number of German settlers, it became saturated with German influence.

With the influx of settlers of mixed ethnicity, disagreements would arise which required a sense of prudence and intuitiveness in order to avoid tragic consequences. Lacking a police force each would seek justice in a manner that pleased them.

"Father once told us of an incident that came about between him and a close neighbor after Father's cow wandered into the neighbor's yard," says Ferdinand. "The enraged neighbor set out to set matters straight. A 'coolness' settled between them. Sensing that prolonged indifference would endanger their relationship, Father apologized. The neighbor accepted but made it clear that if they had not made a truce between them, he had intended to use his newly sharpened ax to settle the dispute. A new set of standards had been set and there was no further incident."

Village life in Volhynia: The small farming village of Jachimufka, in the southeast region of Poland was diverse in its culture. It had a church that was shared by several denominations, a school, a livery stable, and blacksmith shop. The weekly trips to the local church in those days did not include children. During the parents' absence, the eldest child was given the responsibility to care for the younger children and was given chores as well to keep them from wasting time in idle play. Most of the time parents returned to find the household in good order. The Pastor lived in the village among the populous of about two hundred people, along with the Burgermeister (Reeve), and the schoolteacher. The peace of the village prevailed, which was evident by the absence of any police force.

The homes were built with hand-hewn timber making the walls strong and thick. The frame was filled with a mixture of clay and straw that was left to dry and harden in the summer sun. A layer of white plaster was applied to the outer and inner walls. It held the heat in the winter and it was cool in the summer. Roofs made of thatched straw were known to last more than fifty years before they were in need of replacement. Overall people lived a contented, peaceful life.

Flourishing Cultures in Volhynia

The German settlers appeared refined in manner and appearance while the Polish people residing in Volhynia were noticeably more rugged. The Ukrainians who resided there were peaceful. There were also a significant number of Jewish settlers who blended in with the populous and various tribes of Gypsies were also found there. Regardless of the diversity the residents banded together to share their talents and resources while continuing in their own customs and traditions. Infrequent skirmishes resulting from misgivings were settled in the most primitive manner, even though the people needed each other to survive as a community.

The harvest. Every year the harvest brought people together. Since there was no machinery for harvesting large crops, the harvest had to be accomplished by hard labor. Many families who had little means and struggled to survive throughout the year showed up for the harvest to supply needed labor and partake in the harvest feast. As payment for their hard work a banquet of fine food was offered at the end of each day. No one in the village missed working in the harvest as it was considered a time of peace and joy. There was no partiality shown when it came time for the harvest as each farm took their turn in the harvesting work. The farms were harvested one after another from town to town. An abundant harvest meant that all would have a good and prosperous winter. After the work in the harvest was complete, a celebration took place. The harvest celebration was one of the few opportunities for the young people to meet or court. The mothers accompanying their teens to the harvest dance greatly influenced their choice of suitors.

The Economic Unit of Exchange at the Time

The unit of monetary exchange in Poland for the most part was accomplished by bartering; a duty that was left up to the man of the household. This form of commerce suited the life that existed there, but prevented most from accumulating any substantial wealth beyond their immediate needs.

Lorena Lefor Golke

❧

Lorena Lefor was born in Canada, the eldest daughter in a family of eleven children. Lorena began as a youth to write short stories as a hobby. She grew up in Rural Ontario; her first job was delivering the local newspaper in her neighbourhood. It was then that Lorena realized the significance of the writing profession. Having a passion for true human stories, she began many days with a trip to the local library. A brief diversion from her love of the human story took Lorena into the Natural Health field which resulted in publishing of her own Health News journal. Following the death of her husband in 1993, Lorena pursued her writing in earnest by attending the Journalism program at Conestoga College in Kitchener Ontario, a city formerly known as Berlin. Here, she began researching her own ancestry and became interested in the stories told by immigrant families that had been displaced by the Second World War. Throughout her career, Lorena has been a recipient of the Èlsie McGowan award for literary submissions and has written and taught home study courses in the natural health fields in which she is certified. She is presently writing her third novel.

9 781609 760588